TERRITORIES

Territories

A Collection of Linked Stories

Michael Chin

ADVANCE PRAISE

Michael Chin is a literary ring general. He brilliantly renders matches with such detail, such awareness of physical space, that reading this collection feels like sitting in the audience watching the matches live. His ability to create empathy with his characters invites you into the seedy back halls of arenas and asks you to tag along during long hours on the road.

—Quinn Carver Johnson, author of *The Perfect Bastard*

The authenticity of Chin's journey through the greasy minor leagues of pro wrestling is only exceeded by its heart. Punchy, raw, powerful, and real—this book puts you in a chokehold that only gets better the more tightly you're squeezed.

—Chris Koslowski, author of *Kayfabe*

Michael Chin's *Territories* is an immensely readable, remarkably generous collection. I leapt from one story to the next with increasing velocity as I was immersed further in this world. *Territories* is brutal and funny and just so much fun.

—Mike McClelland, author of *Gay Zoo Day*

These sweat-soaked, working-class stories of the desperate and the broke are about busted hearts, swollen muscles, and the kind of economic anxiety that threatens any dreamer worth a damn.

—Matthew Thomas Meade, Author of the short story collections *Strip Mall* and *Rocketflower*

For Riley

CONTENTS

THE ITCH

I started losing my father at the turn of the millennium. It happened the way so many schisms open between dads and daughters—when something comes between them, when something takes a man's place. My mother had just finished chemotherapy—gone into a remission from non-Hodgkin lymphoma in a way that felt permanent in the moment, like we'd never lose her—when I started dating Dylan. It wasn't Dylan that separated me from my father.

It was wrestling.

Dylan's dad watched wrestling. He was, himself, an old wrestler. Not a former wrestler, he'd correct anyone who said it—most of all Dylan's mom—because he said there was no such thing as a truly retired wrestler, and even though his back was broken from a decade and a half in the ring. The latter years had cost him so much time with Dylan as a baby, as a little kid. Hell, I'd lived next door to them my whole life and didn't understand that Dylan had a father until we started talking in grade school, and I learned his dad was more than his mom's friend who came around a few times a month.

The VCR was a boon to Dylan's dad, on the front end of the tape trading enterprise that saw him not only watch the regional wrestling shows, but record them faithfully, then sell or swap them among a network of fellow fans in other locales throughout the country.

New tapes arrived each week, but he re-watched matches and shows that he called *historically important* time and again. "That's Pat Patterson," Dylan's dad pointed at the screen, meaning not the bigger names—Hulk Hogan, Mr. T, Roddy Piper, or Paul Orndorff—in the ring, but rather the gray-haired referee. "People think the referee's only there for window dressing, to make it look more like a legitimate sport. But he has to be in the right place not to block the camera, to act like he doesn't see the heels cheat. And a match like this, Madison Square Garden, a million people watching on closed circuit, and Mr. T doesn't know an arm bar from his asshole—Patterson's directing traffic." He took a bite from his doughnut. Dylan's dad never had a doughnut far from reach, usually plain, cakey ones, though occasionally he'd indulge in Devil's Food or Boston Cream. "People forget how good Pat Patterson was." He gestured his hand at the entire screen, as the camera panned out to capture the full crowd in the arena. The big picture. "A guy like that. He gets the itch for wrestling and it never leaves him. Wrestles twenty, thirty years, then helps with the writing, helps with matches like this."

Dylan's dad had had the itch, too. Maybe he still did those lazy afternoons in front of the TV. He was a talent. A close-call. He worked a handful of matches as a jobber for the big companies—a skilled worker, paid to anonymously take a beating in the ring from bigger stars to make them look like a million bucks. He even had one match that aired nationally, available in the hands of an unknowable number of fellow tape traders. A tag team bout, in which he and the partner he met hours before the match took a shellacking from The Strike Force—Tito Santana before his bull fighter gimmick, Rick Martel before he played a fashion model pretty boy. Dylan's dad didn't like watching that match. Rather than celebrating his most-watched match, he lamented it as the match that closed the door on him ever getting a shot at a full-time deal, at getting to play a cowboy, Indian, or biker himself, relegated instead to a generic singlet or trunks each time one of the big companies booked him. His partner for the match was rough in the ring, awkward and clumsy, and Dylan explained when he showed me the match that that partner had missed the spot where he was supposed to tag in his father, thus costing him his opportunity to shine, thus meaning the powers that be lumped him in as no more talented than the jabroni he was teamed with.

I was less interested in Dylan's dad's work or the 1970s and 1980s than what was happening in the moment. What would become known as The Attitude Era.

\#

The Attitude Era. Late nineties, early two-thousands. Steve Austin hitting the Stone Cold Stunner on The Rock, The Undertaker throwing Mick Foley off the roof of Hell in a Cell, and sultry Sable becoming a villainess in live TV because she spoke the precise truth that *the women want to be me, and the men come to see me.*

There was something more to wrestling than half-naked people rolling on the mat in staged combat, and never was it more palpable than the Attitude Era. This was the time when wrestling became water cooler talk in offices, when kids unabashedly wore wrestling t-shirts to school because it translated to anyone with a pulse.

I wanted to taste a moment of what Triple H and Eddie Guerrero and Jeff Hardy all must have felt at that time.

\#

Dylan and I started wrestling when we were younger, when we really were just friends. We tried holds. What kind of best friends didn't try out the Sharpshooter, the camel clutch on one another? We discovered the figure four leglock did hurt, though it was near impossible to apply without the benefit of a willing victim. We discovered the cross-face chicken wing was, in fact, deadly; that the bearhug required more force than the wrestling on TV would have you believe; that the Boston crab was mostly harmless if you bent with it, unless the person applying the hold put the pressure on the recipient's neck like Chris Jericho did.

We graduated from experimenting with holds to a mix of actually grappling and collaborating to recreate sequences from Bret Hart vs. The British Bulldog and Shawn Michaels vs. The Undertaker.

Our parents told us to stop when they caught us. I'm sure some of it had to do with thinking we'd hurt each other, but particularly when Dylan's mom broke us up, I got the distinct sense she was more concerned about a sweaty teenage boy grabbing a sweaty teenage girl, bodies all squeezing and friction against one another on his bedroom floor.

To be fair, we did end up making out for the first time when we were wrestling.

\#

Wrestling was dangerous. Even the disclaimers at the starts of shows warned us not to try it at home.

I choked out Dylan one time, when we were wrestling more competitively. Just after we started necking, just when our bodies had grown big enough to be dangerous. Big enough he gave me a head start. Let me start on top of him or start with a hold applied. I put him in a triangle choke hold I'd picked from a tape of Japanese wrestling, threading his neck and arm between my legs, thighs collapsed around him, my right foot in my left knee pit, not least of all choking him with his own arm itself. As much as we had hurt each other—accidentally or on purpose—Dylan was never willing to tap out to a girl, so he got choked and choked until he really was out, and I asked my father for help because I was worried I'd killed him. Dad lifted Dylan's legs in the air to get the blood flowing to his brain and he woke up in a few seconds. I felt sheepish, figuring he'd probably have woken up on his own without the intervention and I'd needlessly let Dad in on that we'd been wrestling.

\#

Dylan and I started frequenting the tennis court. It started with tennis—really, it did—when Dylan's mom found a pair of old rackets when she was cleaning out the attic and bought us a roll of balls from Walmart and suggested we play. Minimal attempt to mask that she was posing an alternative to wrestling. Something else athletic that even involved hitting something to relieve our teenage energy reserves, without the same implications of sex or violence. So we took the rackets and balls to the park a half-mile from our street. I expected we'd take turns trying to hit the balls at birds, or over the fence at passersby until all the balls were suitably lost, then go home and say we'd tried.

But that fence. I'd never noticed it until we went to play, but then I really saw it—twenty by thirty, maybe twelve feet tall, all steel mesh. No fence at all.

Our very own steel cage.

I don't know how else to describe it but love at first sight.

We placed the rackets down. We wrestled. There was a sense of play, bordering on make believe, in remaking this place in our image. But even from that initial play, I had visions of what this space was itching to be.

#

We came back every day. Spent hours. Mercifully, no one came to play tennis. We started taking down the net altogether, because it only got in our way, and then stopped putting it back up. No sign that anyone cared. No sign anyone put it back up. I liked Dylan's theory that maybe people played tennis when we weren't around, then took the net back down to restore our disorder.

#

We kept up the pretense of bringing our racquets and balls. Even went so far as to bounce balls to dirty them and leave one behind every few days to sell the idea we really were playing tennis. Dylan's mom bought us a fresh roll of balls and complimented us on our suntans. Dad asked which of us he should call Venus, which Serena when we told him we were going back to the court.

\#

Dylan caught word from one of his guy friends who worked at a hotel that they'd thrown away a whole floor's worth of mattresses. We borrowed another friend's pickup and drove to the landfill to recover them. We drove them back in fives, tied down with bungee cords I found in our basement, until we filled that tennis court with our own mats, until, despite Dylan still hedging, he watched me climb up to the crossbeam of the cage, six feet up, and caught me when I dove down. It wasn't a picture-perfect cross body block, but I dare say it was a hell of a lot better than we'd managed with my leaps from the pitiful heights of a bed, a couch, and with nothing softer than a shag rug to break our fall.

\#

That first dive, I felt reassured. We could realize my vision.

\#

We drew up flyers, advertising Cage Wrestling War, coming to a location to be announced soon. I'd thought it through. Don't give enough lead time for anyone to go looking at the park and asking questions about permits and old mattresses in the tennis court. We hooked an audience, though, emphasizing wrestling and a free show and Shermantown. No entertainment ever came to Shermantown, least of all free.

Dylan's dad made mention he'd heard about a show coming. That got me nervous, until his old-time wrestling fan instincts kicked in. No names on the card. *Probably a bunch of backwoods hillbillies punching each other for real. No thanks.*

\#

We watched cage matches for research. Bret Hart vs. Owen Hart at SummerSlam 1994 in the greatest bloodless cage match ever. I wanted to bleed a little to make our match worth the while. But Dylan said no blood—at least not intentionally.

There were limits. He had to have his way sometimes.

\#

Dylan's dad showed us his favorite match from the last few years. No cage, but a man and a woman. Referee Bill Alfonso vs. valet Beulah McGillicutty. It was a bad bootleg tape wavy lines cutting through the picture three or four times each minute.

It was no technical masterpiece. But it was a believable fight. Dylan's dad said that, in real life, Alfonso was on the outs with the company. That he wrestled at all was his make-good—an apology, a comeuppance, a proving ground that he was worth keeping employed. Neither he nor Beulah knew how to wrestle, but they brawled with intensity, hitting one another hard, doing their best takes on wrestling moves men twice their respective body weights did in more traditional matches. Intense enough to believe it was a real fight—the clumsy way that neither quite knew how to use their limbs in combat only enhanced the effect.

They sweated and even cried, but not because they were soft. Because they were gritting their teeth and fighting through submission holds.

\#

Dylan and I started to itch. Lying in the middle of our steel cage following an afternoon session, sweating, breathing hard, my calf crossed over his shin, he admitted the undeniable truth out loud. "I think the mattresses have bugs."

Of course there was a reason the hotel had discarded mattresses wholesale.

Of course we wouldn't stop.

\#

We watched the classic. The cage match everyone talks about when they talk about cage matches.

Madison Square Garden. Don Muraco, the statuesque hulk billed as "The Rock" before Dwayne Johnson commandeered the moniker. Jimmy "Superfly" Snuka, the barefoot Fijian wrestling with an island wild man gimmick. Muraco won, but it's the aftermath everyone remembers. In his righteous indignation, Snuka dragged Muraco back into the cage, battered him to incapacitation and left him sprawled on the middle of the mat. Superfly scaled the cage, flashed the universal hand signal to say "I love you," to the fans, then leapt all the way off the top to crush his rival's broken body.

History is a liar. People will tell you Snuka won the match with that splash, but the final bell had already rung—it wasn't the winning maneuver, but rather an act of vengeance after Snuka lost. It also wasn't the first time someone leapt off the top of a cage; Snuka did it a year earlier, a bad guy then, except the hero, Bob Backlund rolled out of the way, only to escape the cage and win.

But here, Snuka hit the splash. Here, Snuka was the hero. In an era when no one had flipped backward into a moonsault or flung anybody with their legs in a hurricanrana, or put someone through a table, Snuka was the innovator of violence. Muraco was the man who trusted him enough to lay still and take the ultimate blow.

I backed up the video to watch him leap again and again and again.

"You're not doing that," Dylan said.

Again.

\#

We advertised an intergender wrestling match. A little extra intrigue to draw an audience, complete with a photo of me and of Dylan, each with the brightness turned way down via the magic of the image software on the library computers. We were little more than silhouettes, an eye here, an arm there, enough to sell that I was thin and might be attractive. Enough to communicate that he was bigger and this might be a mismatch and what red-blooded wrestling fan could turn away from the spectacle?

We'd have to come up with names. It wouldn't do us very well to try to fly under the police and parental radar to broadcast our real names for everyone to hear.

I made the decision.

"You'll be Hansel," I said. Innocent. Boyish. A hero to undermine expectations about a young man doing combat with a young woman.

"I suppose that makes you Gretel?" he asked.

"No," I said. "I'm The Witch."

\#

We picked out theme music.

I chose "Paradise City" by Guns 'n' Roses. I'd dated another boy, in between spells with Dylan, who idolized Axl Rose and grew out his hair to look something like him. This song was my main takeaway from our few weeks together. I remember his comment, as the opening played in his garage, that a human being couldn't hear that initial kick drum and not have it *pump your nads*. Never mind that I didn't have nads. I understood when my body couldn't help but rock to the sound. The power.

#

We drew a crowd. It was hard to tell park-goers from people who'd come for our match at first, when teenagers showed up with brown paper bags they may just as easily have been coming to our match as expecting to have a drink during a sleepy Saturday night at the park.

But they all surrounded the cage. Full-on grownups, too. Some kids with their parents, because maybe they took wrestling to be synonymous with the kind of wrestling Dylan and I had grown up on of Hillbilly Jim hip tossing Ravishing Rick Rude, then dosey-doe-ing with Mean Gene Okerlund in celebration.

But maybe because they'd come to see us. Maybe because of the flyers. Maybe because their curiosity lured them to us, away from their original intentions in coming to play at the park.

Maybe because nothing attracts a crowd like a crowd.

There had to have been a hundred people in the grass surrounding the tennis court.

We crouched on the far side of the bathrooms that had been marked out of order for as long as I could remember. Dylan stripped down to his tank top and pulled up the long, shin-covering socks meant for soccer, that night meant to simulate the length and look of wrestling boots. I wore a black thrift-store dress, skirt slit high so I could move, over a black one-piece, something like what an old school lady wrestler would wear.

I wrestled barefoot. Like an old school wrestler who couldn't afford boots. Like Jimmy Snuka.

I'd burned a two-track CD of our songs—a waste of a disc not to fill the seventy minutes available, but I didn't want to risk playing the wrong track. I loaded new C batteries to fit the boom box my father blared music from while he worked on his car in the garage.

It had sounded so loud in the garage.

It didn't sound like much in the open air of the park, hardly audible over the chatter surrounding the cage, talking, laughing, speculating about what they were about to see. Dylan had to elbow his path to the cage door as our fans began to take notice the show had started.

Dylan looked small. And nervous.

I was smaller. But I was coming to the cage after Dylan. No reason not to bring the boom box with me. Its energy. Its noise. Its kick drum. I got a smattering of cheers. It got louder when I started climbing the cage.

I'd decided I'd enter over the top, and hadn't warned Dylan about it because I knew he'd try to talk me out of the extra risk of hurting myself before the match began.

I didn't factor in how hard it would be to climb one handed, the other still carrying the boom box. Adrenaline got me to the cross beam, but I was struggling with balance and my left climbing hand throbbed from the effort of holding on and supporting the disproportionate weight of my body.

Another ad lib: I threw the boom box, as hard as I could, over the heads of the onlookers beneath me, crashing broken to the grass behind them.

Louder cheers.

Dylan looked worried. When I got to the top of the cage he positioned himself, as if to catch me if I fell. As if to catch me if I jumped.

But I climbed, swung one leg over the top, then the next and scaled down, light and easy then as the cheers shifted from excitement over "Paradise City" and the crash and the climb to anticipation of the fight.

And there we were, just like we planned it, each standing in a different mattress, each standing against opposite corners of the cage. Dylan gave me a look that asked, *do you really want to go through with this?*

I nailed him with the enzuguiri we'd planned. A little stiffer than we'd planned.

I played the stick-and-move offense of the outsized wrestler. Leap frog, drop down, arm drag, drop kick, drop kick, drop kick, back into the corner into the monkey flip.

Dylan took over on the heat segment. The bigger body clamping me in a bear hug, transitioning into a sleeper hold, then an abdominal stretch. These were known as rest holds. Time for the wrestlers to rest our bodies, only acting as though these squeezes and contortions hurt. Rest for the fans so they might quiet and be ready to pop when the action started again in earnest.

Dylan applied the Human Torture Rack. I leapt into position, timed to his lift, up onto him, stretched across his neck and shoulders, my spine bent. It did hurt a little, but mostly it was a challenge not to escape the hold—to writhe while maintaining balance rather than sending us both crashing to the mattresses.

Then the comeback. The punches to his gut. The punches to his face, the first landing a lot harder than I'd meant, but what could I do? The crowd was rocking. There was blood. My knuckles. His forehead. I didn't know the point of origin. I knew I had to keep going.

We moved into the closing sequence. I scaled the cage.

I was supposed to climb as high as the crossbeam and dive off. Dylan could take the blow. He'd catch me as he fell backward, as I fell forward, as we threatened to break through the stuffing of the mattress below. It would be a good ending.

I climbed higher.

Dylan called after me. First a *hey* and then a *get back down here* and then some sort of taunt, keeping with our roles as competing wrestlers, something I couldn't quite hear because the crowd was getting louder and I was getting higher. He called my name.

I reached the top.

A hand signal. The international sign for *I love you* to Dylan and to the people who'd come to see us and to the police siren I first heard in that moment and to the flash of red and blue light, all bound to break us up, but I loved it for coming too late and for the chaos it added.

I leapt. Body at full extension. Flying higher into the sky, thirteen, fourteen, feet up before I peaked and started coming down.

I imagined my father, who wasn't there, who didn't understand wrestling, who might have worried about me breaking my neck. I imagined Dylan's father, too. Talking about the itch. Recognizing that in this moment, I scratched it.

I crashed, bumpy skin on bumpy skin, sweat on sweat, blood on blood and puss and spit and bone and love.

THE EMPEROR

When I left home to become a professional wrestler, Mom didn't want me to go.

She told me the things so many wrestlers hear before they're wrestlers about how I was going to break my neck and that I should go to college instead. Did I really think I could live out of a suitcase on the road and what kind of life was rolling around mats with other sweaty women while men leered at me and Aunt Loretta could get me a job answering phones at her office and what was I thinking and didn't I love her and how could I make this choice and—

Dad told her to let me go. He didn't so much as turn down the TV or get up from his recliner or look my way, duffel bag over my shoulder, car keys in hand, wearing a ratty old Bret "The Hitman" Hart t-shirt with the neck cut to a wide V. I can't imagine either of them recognized any symbolism in me wearing the shirt of my favorite wrestler—this small salute to his legend, this small prayer to the wrestling deities for safe passage and good luck on my way out of Shermantown, New York.

Dad said to let me go. He said the sooner I left, the sooner I could come home.

\#

I learned that to "go home," in the parlance of wrestling, was to end the match. You go home after someone hits their finisher, sure, or sometimes off a flash pin out of nowhere, sometimes succumbing to a submission hold or passing out to a sleeper. There are double count outs and double disqualifications, even double pins sometimes. Time limit draws are out of vogue, the audience's attention span too short.

#

I went to a training camp, the only woman in my cohort, so I had to practice shoulder blocks and hammerlocks and float overs and slams with bodies bigger, stronger, hairier than my own.

A bald guy, the hairiest back of them all, said he didn't want to wrestle a girl. I hit him hard.

I hit everyone hard, taking to heart the guidance of our trainer that the hits had to be real or the fans would see right through them. The art was in bodies working together, bending, falling, responding to every pressure ten-fold.

I learned to hit the men I trusted the hardest, because I learned what they could take.

I'd learn to hit the ones I love the hardest. Because they can take it. Because they can forgive.

#

There's a story my mother told me when I was young. Her mother-in-law was critical when I was first born. She said that Mom let me cry too long, too much without comforting me. She shared the folktale of the The Taker, a monster who came when babies cried too long unattended, under the rationale that if no one cared enough to pick up the child, she was fair game.

It was a ridiculous story, of course, but in Mom's sleep-deprived state, the story rattled her. She took to hardly ever setting me down at all, even keeping me on her shoulder when she wielded a sharp knife to cut raw potatoes for stew or stirred the hot broth on the stove. The silver lining: she'd made me feel safe, attached.

She told me the story when I was old enough to recognize she was more attached to me than I was to her. Not that I didn't love her, but she was neurotic and needy and never wanted to let go.

She told me that story when I was too young. I didn't take away that Grandma was crazy. I took away The Taker. The image I conjured in my mind, fifty percent Grim Reaper, fifty percent Frankenstein Monster, one hundred percent hiding in the shadows whenever I was left alone and particularly after I turned off the light in my room at night.

\#

Mom cried over the phone, asking when I'd come home. I heard Dad in the background, telling her not to cry. *You have to let her go.*

\#

I didn't see it coming when I got the call to head out to my first territory. Damphry.

The first thing you need to know if you're going to wrestle in Damphry is not to cross The Emperor. Case in point—1998, when The Emperor caught wind Wild Bill

Grady meant to jump to the big leagues and leave Southern Fried Wrestling hanging without its champion.

The Emperor—Akio Fujinami—was legendary by then for spitting fireballs. It was a trick of flash paper and slipping lighter fluid into his mouth and spewing flame. The gimmick was a spectacle, and it was safe—he must have done it a thousand times without serious harm to himself or his opponents. But Bill Grady?

Have you heard a three-hundred-pound man cry?

Have you seen him disfigured and clutching at his melted flesh?

According to the denizens of Damphry, you want no part of The Emperor's fury.

"Go to Damphry," my trainer, Lily Lance, said. She'd been in wrestling herself almost as long as The Emperor. She had liver-spotted skin that made her look older than she was. Every word she said elbowed its way through a cloud of cigarette smoke. Early on, I thought the smoke made her look mystical. But everything that looked supernatural in the wrestling world was more smoke and mirrors than magic. I knew all that going in. I understood it by the time I was leaving her for The Emperor.

"Go to Damphry," she repeated. "You won't learn technique, but you've already got that. You'll learn showmanship. You'll learn *heat*."

So, I went.

#

Millions of fireflies invaded that summer. Damphry always had some, but there were now swarms of them, flying like torches across the night air, lighting up the sidewalk outside bar row after last call, finding their way through cracked windows and into bedrooms at night. Everywhere flight, everywhere light.

\#

Fujinami wasn't just the long-standing top star and often-times champion of SFW (eighty-four reigns to date and he was challenging for the title again at the end of the month when I arrived) but he was also the majority owner, promoter, and booker of the territory. That meant he decided most of who stayed and went, who won and lost matches. He was a goddamn local institution, not just famous, but tight with police and slum lords and doctors and mechanics and reporters and hairdressers and school officials and the mayor's office. Anybody who was anybody in Damphry.

He owned the Lucky Dragon, too. A genuine shithole with fat cockroaches dotting the floor, and some of the shittiest Chinese food on the planet. Everything chewy and deep-fried grade D meat, slathered in hot sauce that, to be generous, approximated sweet and sour or General Tso's. But wrestlers ate free, so it served its purpose.

Wrestlers ate free, so the Lucky Dragon drew a crowd every night because the citizens of Damphry loved wrestling and if they could bump elbows with the boys, they'll sure as hell have dinner there.

\#

The free eats were one reason for a wrestler to aspire to Damphry There was also the convenience of travel, the central location. Move to Damphry and you were at the focal point of a fifty-mile radius of other small towns to wrestle in on a loop, month after month. The SFW office sits on Main Street, right next door to the Lucky Dragon.

#

The Emperor was not Chinese.

Rabbit Johnson schooled me while we waited for The Emperor at his hole-in-the-wall office—a narrow room with a desk, lit by the restaurant next door and its neon sign that read *laundry* in Chinese characters. Fujinami bought it from a laundromat when it was going out of business a decade ago, certain no local could read what it meant. Why bother with overhead lights in the office, when the bright neon lights outside The Emperor's other business could illuminate the place enough to do the business of a regional wrestling promotion? We sat on a futon with a badly ripped cloth cover, foam mattress innards peeking through, the wooden frame creaking every time either one of us shifted our position.

The other rooms of the little building were for merchandise storage, mostly t-shirts The Emperor had wrestlers drive from town to town for him. There was also a bench press and dumbbells no one but The Emperor was allowed to touch. Rabbit warned me about that, as if I could see the weights, as if I had a mind to sneak in a workout then and there.

"He opened a Chinese restaurant because working people like Chinese food and it's cheap." Rabbit was a wrestler himself and wore the tell-tale too-tight t-shirt over bleached blue jeans and snakeskin cowboy boots. "It's a rib on white people anyway—because he knows they can't tell the difference between Japanese, Chinese, and Korean anyway. He knows nobody's going to call him a fraud."

There were banners on the wall, just behind the desk, with metallic writing that almost shimmered in the lamp light. To Rabbit's point, I didn't know if they were Chinese characters or Japanese or something else altogether.

\#

The Emperor was American. Born and raised in Damphry, when it wasn't quite so Podunk, back before the one-two punch of the town light bulb factory going out of business and a soft drink company moving on to greener pastures. It was still a small southern town, where people made squinty eyes at Fujinami and asked if he knew karate, until he did sign up for karate classes and started not only getting into but winning fights. At eighteen, he round-housed a wrestler who was bullying him at a bar, and got an offer to join the team.

That was all a long time ago.

\#

I'd come to learn years later that everyone had spent time in Damphry. A badge of honor. A rite of passage, a trial to withstand—like most things, it all depended on whom you asked.

"Forget technique and your flippity-floppities," Jimmy Jack James, one of the wrestlers who trained me, told me before I left. He referred to any move that called for one or both wrestlers to leave both feet a *flippity-floppity*. "In Damphry they punch and they kick, and they grab headlocks. You want something flashier than that, it'd better be your finisher."

\#

Though The Emperor used variations on his roundhouse kick to finish opponents early in his career, he gave up using martial arts strikes before long, not wanting to get pigeonholed into Asian stereotypes.

Kung fu wrestlers are mid-carders, he'd explain when he was disposed to offer up wisdom from his career. The Emperor learned to throw great big overhand punches—the kind that would never work in a real fight. Just the same, the kind of blows fans could see from the cheap seats. He built anticipation with every wind up.

His signature finisher was a sit-out powerbomb that he called the Grave Digger.

\#

The Damphry Civic Center was a dump. It was a little arena that I heard had hosted an array of local sports teams that came and went, mostly going because there came some point when their schedule or scoreboard, or the condition they'd left the locker room in came into conflict with The Emperor.

The arena was for wrestling. The occasional convention for organizers who played nice—taking care of the space, acting obsequiously, and often as not making some arrangement to pay The Emperor to make an appearance, having the Lucky Dragon provide catering, or for the privilege of touting the arena as the home of Southern Fried Wrestling.

By default, the ring stayed up from week to week. A hard ring, with dead spots that didn't have as much give or that threatened to give way beneath the weight of a body. The ring ropes weren't rope at all, but rather garden hoses wrapped in electrical tape, meaning only the most sure-footed visiting luchador would fly.

Most wrestling companies brought rings when they traveled, but SFW was the exception. It was written into contracts to have a ring waiting for us, and most of the rings were nicer than the one at our home arena—newer, cleaner, more solidly built, if only because The Emperor would complain and threaten not to come back if the ring wasn't up to snuff. Then there were the towns we did bring a ring to—*we* in the sense that it was all hands on deck to transport the parts and to help with set up the afternoon before such a show. The Emperor charged a premium—separate fees for providing, setting up, and taking down the ring. These practices weren't unique to him as a promoter, but those of us doing the labor never saw our payouts change for the extra hours worked, for the extra money coming in.

#

Rabbit warned me never to get caught alone with The Emperor. Least of all after hours, or after he'd been drinking.

I could read between the lines when Rabbit gave me this advice because I was a girl, and a girl whom might be considered pretty, at least by the standards of women who got punched in the face on a regular basis. I rarely let myself be alone with a man from the wrestling business. I'd been watching Rabbit's long fingers for any sign he meant to touch me.

When The Emperor arrived, he was bigger than I'd expected. That's the thing about the wrestling business.

Everyone's big, so by comparison hardly anyone looks that big at all. Take a guy like The Emperor, only 5'9", 5'10", maybe two-twenty-five and he looked like an everyday joe who'd sooner be working in an insurance office than wrestling.

In person, The Emperor's hands were enormous. I stood up to shake his hand and watched mine disappear.

"Rabbit been takin good care of you?"

I told him he had, as Rabbit and I sat back down on the futon and The Emperor pulled out his leather office chair from the desk. He was wearing a dark blue suit, his collar loose like he was at the end of his workday.

There was an old school desktop computer, complete with a CRT monitor and CPU that took up half his desk. A printer hard-wired in, my contract waiting in the tray.

He'd gone over the terms with me on the phone. Standard issue. No days off, except for injury—confirmed by a doctor, paid for by the wrestler. Complete submission to the office's creative control of my character. Base pay, plus a percentage of gates, though the promoter had no obligation to tell wrestlers what any of the gates were.

A lot of promoters didn't bother to put it all in writing. A lot of wrestlers didn't bother to ask. I thought that spoke well of The Emperor and signed without reading it all. A show of trust. The Emperor liked that.

"Let's get you something to eat."

#

The Emperor took my photo before we left the office that first time, after I'd signed over the next year of my life to his discretion. He printed out a black-and-white copy that stretched across a 8.5 x 11 sheet of paper, and brought it next door to the restaurant to tack to the wall in an empty space amidst thirty-something other headshots. He gave me a red Sharpie and had me sign. I figured the pictures were for the fans to marvel at. I'd learn that, like any opportunity to make someone or something pull double duty, the photos were there, too, to confirm wrestlers' identities for the staff, so they'd know it was OK to feed them whatever they wanted.

After The Emperor and Rabbit, the first SFW wrestler I met was Tully Anderson, a guy who'd made his rounds and had a cup of coffee in WWE, but explained he'd moved to Damphry to settle down some in a place that'd be good for his daughter. "Here with salt-of-the-earth people, where she won't get a bunch of wooly-headed liberal ideas dancing in her head."

He had his daughter Silly—short for Priscilla—for the summer. She was seventeen, eighteen at the end of summer, and I got the distinct impression that her mother had sent her off to slow the momentum of worse influences back home.

"And check this out." Tully held up a mason jar, three fireflies trapped inside, one flying from one side of the glass to another, flickering its light every now and again , the other two more sluggish. "The two of us caught them together at dusk. Pretty cool, right?"

Silly rolled her eyes. She rolled her eyes at half of what Tully said, a lot of dad jokes and references to things the two of them might do together this summer, like teaching her how to fish, and taking her to the great big doll store the next town over, and going to the father-daughter dance in the fall, if he could convince Silly's mother to let her stay long enough.

"I'll have school by then." She picked out peas and chunks of carrots to eat from her fried rice, unlike me using chopsticks, and Tully who left his fork sitting at the side of his plate in favor of picking up dumplings and water chestnuts between his thumb and forefinger.

"She's studious, this one." Tully tried to put a hand on her shoulder, but she shrank from him until the distance was awkward and he snapped his fingers in the air, as if that's all he'd meant to do all along. "She's going to college next year."

"That's wonderful," I said. "What'll you study?"

She shrugged. It was a small mercy, then, when a mother and son came to the table, the boy too shy to ask for Tully's autograph, the mom extending one of the black-and-white programs The Emperor sold for a buck a pop. Tully signed, and suggested they get my signature, too, to be the first in town to get an autograph from a new talent, and then that they get Silly's autograph, because out of all of us, she was the one who was really going to be somebody someday.

Before they could agree, Tully swung his arm to give Silly the program in grand fashion. His big forearm caught the mason jar and sent it off the table, crashing to floor, all sparkling shards, Tully cursing, the mom covering her kid's ears, the fireflies flying free.

#

My first match, I worked Casey Heart, who wrestled in a neon pink unitard and was billed from Calgary, Alberta, Canada—with the suggestion she was connected to the famous Hart wrestling family of Stu, Bret, Owen, et al. The gimmick wasn't getting over with the fans, which was a shame because she was pretty good with her jiu jitsu-informed offense of arm bars and chokes that passed for technical wrestling, with the added wrinkle that anyone who knew real fighting could see that if she actually torqued any of her holds, she really could hurt someone.

I finished her with a German suplex into a rolling bridge. Afterward, The Emperor would tell me in the locker room that that finisher was too complex. "Keep it simple, silly." He slapped my ass, as if by way of punctuation.

Silly was with him there, and she laughed. Silly, the only one not in spandex. The Emperor didn't like non-wrestlers in the locker rooms, least of all kids, but to hear the bustle backstage, after he met Silly, he went out of his way to invite her come see how things looked behind the scenes.

But I recognized the way The Emperor stood over her, bare chested, a casual lean, hand to a wall, arm supporting at just the right angle to flex without looking as though he were trying to flex. I recognized in her, too, the short shorts, the blouse carefully unbuttoned low, the little cross necklace that suggested a sort of virginal virtue, daring the boy she looked up to through fluttering eyelashes to tear it loose.

Rabbit warned Tully, "Watch your girl."

Maybe that's why Tully came to me.

\#

If you lived in Damphry you came to learn firefly trivia that summer.

For example, you learned a firefly couldn't burn you. Theirs was a cold light.

There was speculation that given fireflies spent a year-plus underground before they took flight, they had arrived in secret the year before, only to make themselves known now, Trojan horsed in the soil, patiently waiting.

You learned that even before they hatched, firefly eggs glowed too.

\#

Tully asked me to protect Silly, because protecting her himself would've been too obvious.

Too obvious to Silly, and *damn it, I'm not blind. I know she doesn't want to listen to me.*

Too obvious to the Emperor. *He doesn't care that I'm her father. The only way he'd care is if I were willing to help him get in her pants, and for Chrissake, she's seventeen years old.*

So, I helped. Within limits. Silly didn't have the same levels of contempt or distrust around me, as a woman, and more to the point, as someone who wasn't her father, Being new made it easier to play dumb when I lingered around her, like a friend, maybe a third wheel to her and the Emperor, but a third wheel that could keep them from balancing the axel of their two wheels into a smooth ride. I'd ask the Emperor questions to keep him occupied as well until the locker room filled up with more bodies, more obstacles.

I'm not sure when the switch flipped, but before too long, I found the Emperor watching me closer. How much of my bad timing could be chalked up to coincidence, to an oblivious new girl?

\#

Fireflies lined the biggest tree in Damphry, an out of place fir tree the town planted some decades before. However momentarily, the bugs lined up to form perfect circles. Long enough for passersby to take pictures because it looked like a Christmas tree, there in the hottest, most humid part of summer.

#

One of those times, lingering around Silly, I got a look at her on her laptop computer, submitting her senior quote for her high school yearbook.

She invoked Neil Young. "It's better to burn out than to fade away."

#

The Emperor made a big deal about Silly's eighteenth birthday. I got the impression that birthdays weren't ordinarily special, not least of all when Rabbit's came and went with a smattering of well wishes, with a handful of the boys going drinking after a show.

But for Silly, the Emperor declared we would put on a show. She got to pick the main event—who would compete and the stipulations. I could only imagine that he assumed Silly would pick him, maybe opposite her father, maybe opposite a top contender like The Kaleidoscope Warrior.

Instead, she picked me.

The Emperor let her have a live mic in the ring to announce the match in front of the Damphry crowd two weeks out. That was rare in wrestling—for someone to make an announcement when management didn't know what she'd say in advance. It was sure as hell the only time I heard of anything like it in Damphry.

But I'd face Geri the Giant, a redhead who stood a legit six-foot-eight in her bare feet, billed as a seven-footer, referred to alternately as an Amazon and a monster by the announcers at ringside.

And Silly, whom I hadn't seen show any glimmer of interest in wrestling when her father introduced her around or tried to show her holds and reversals or talk wrestling history, nonetheless ran her tongue over her lips and finished with a smile, "in a steel cage match."

#

A pair of women approached me at the Lucky Dragon that night. The crowd at the restaurant was always biggest the night of a show, when it was one of the few places open late and when there were sure to be wrestlers to mingle with, standing room only, more like a wedding reception than a typical restaurant experience.

The restaurant served from small, disposable containers on show night under the twin premises that the dish washers couldn't keep up with the customers, and they were easier to hold in your hand. Rabbit filled me in that it was really a matter of shortchanging the customers. Sell enough undersized containers of Kung Pao Chicken and you'd save a whole serving or two or ten. Saving food. Compelling customers, still waiting to talk to their favorite wrestlers, to buy more to eat because they were still hungry and weren't going home anytime soon.

The women who came to me didn't seem to have much trouble asserting their will, bumping through crowds, zeroing in on who they wanted to talk to. They both looked fiftyish, one's hair dyed maroon, the other blond, each wearing different Emperor t-shirts. The blond said that I must have done something to make The Emperor really mad.

I asked her what she was talking about.

"Sweetheart, I know you're new here, but we don't have a lot of cage matches. And Geri the Giant's not just a name. She's *enormous*."

Her friend chimed in. "She's going to eat you alive, buttercup."

I'd learned, those first couple weeks in the territory, that the lines between fans eager to lose themselves in our wrestling drama and full-on marks who took it for granted that what they saw in the ring was one-hundred-percent real were razor thin and fluid.

"It wasn't the Emperor who made the match," I said. "It was—the girl." I tripped over that last part. The Emperor had presented her as just another fan, not a wrestler's daughter, posing it as goodwill that she'd been given the chance to match-make for her birthday.

"Honey, ain't nothing goes down in Damphry without The Emperor's endorsement," Maroon said. "That girl was the messenger, plain and simple."

I nodded along. Put on the combination of trepidation and courage that seemed appropriate to my character. It wasn't until after they'd left that I found myself standing across the way from Geri, talking to another fan, that I started to wonder if the two women with the warning were right.

\#

I didn't realize that a cage match meant an outdoor show. The Emperor stored the cage at a local warehouse, owned by a fan all too eager to do the wrestlers a favor. The Emperor stored it there because it wouldn't fit in his office or his home. It wouldn't fit in the arena either.

So, the show took place in the high school football stadium, ordinarily reserved for big, climactic shows that would draw larger crowds. The steel cage was, itself, a draw, though, not to mention that from what I heard there'd never been a women's cage match in Damphry before.

#

Fireflies, as we recognize them, in their glowing adult form, only live for about two months, and that's if they survive their natural predators like birds, spiders, and frogs. Fireflies are known to eat each other sometimes, too.

#

Geri looked nervous before the show. The two of us walked up to, and then on the stack of four sides of the steel cage that would be erected around the ring and clamped together for our main event. I was going to win, climbing up and over the top to escape the cage. In the past, cages were meant to keep everyone else out, to leave the two wrestlers to battle it out until one finished the other. In these modern times, fans wanted to see the climb—for one wrestler to scale impossibly high before descending back to the masses, somewhere between fallen angel and superhero.

Winning a cage match that early in my tenure was a good sign. I might be a champion before long.

I knelt down and slapped a hand against the center of the mesh, establishing the sweet spot in the cage for Geri to slam my head against early on, so the most fans could see it, so the cage would rattle its loudest. Hit the sweet spot and the fans would question if I'd make it out alive.

#

A ticket got everyone in attendance a slice of birthday cake. The Emperor had gotten a big one donated by Chewy's Bakery, across the street from the Lucky Dragon. A big, tiered devil's food cake. The kind any wrestling fan would have been conditioned to expect some mystery wrestler to pop out of at just the right time and launch an attack, were it not for the sureness with which the Emperor sliced through the icing to remove the first piece. Were it not for the fact that the cake was gone by the time the opening bell rang, enough fans in attendance to consume it all.

#

Silly didn't want cake. She said she'd get fat.
The Emperor smeared frosting on her nose.

#

The crowd waited after the penultimate match, through the set up of the cage—longer than some of the undercard matches themselves. The other wrestlers carried the cage walls and held them steady, as the stagehands fumbled with clamps they hardly ever used.

It was the biggest audience I'd ever had for a match. The Emperor claimed, on the house mic, an attendance of five thousand, though no one checked his numbers, and the wrestlers all assumed he'd exaggerated. It was my first proper main event—the opportunity to close a show, and the fans stayed there to watch, even after they'd emptied their beer cups and the cotton candy had long since dissolved on the children's tongues, and all that was left in the popcorn tubs were the dry kernels that had never blossomed.

The match went as planned. I ran and rolled and jumped to keep away. The classic rope-a-dope waiting for Geri the Giant to tire herself out from chasing me, or to run face first into the cage off of a charge and give me an opening.

Then she went for a choke slam.

The choke slam has two parts.

The first is a work. The goozle—catching me by the throat in what looks like a choke, but is really more placing her hand under my chin—followed by the lift, which is more a matter of me jumping in the air than her lifting me by my neck.

The slam is real. Maybe Geri didn't throw me down as hard as she could, but falling flat from a height of six-feet-plus—there's no faking that. She knocked the air out of me, and I only just barely caught my breath before she dropped an elbow on my chest.

The heat was on. When Geri slammed my head against the cage, I noticed Silly and The Emperor sitting on the far side, in the front row. It was rare for The Emperor to sit among the people, but Silly's birthday was a special occasion.

He had his hand on her leg.

Geri put her sweaty hand on my leg, applying a half crab. Part of the psychology for a giant in a cage match is to work the leg and limit the hero's ability to climb, to have any hope of escape.

But I fought back.

Sweat flying with every connection of a forearm to Geri's chest. Then a dropkick. Pause to sell that my knee was hurt, that I should have known better than to go leaping in the air, then grit my teeth and come at her again with a flurry, all leading up to a sleeper hold.

Geri's arm flailed for the ropes, desperation setting in.

This was the finish.

The sleeping giant prone on the mat, I made my climb.

I climbed up The Emperor and Silly's side of the cage. I only paused for a second when I notice that his hand had slid up her leg, up her skirt.

It was a short skirt to begin with.

She didn't have her legs crossed, not the way women do on instinct. She sat with her legs open, girlish.

I tried not to react.

I climbed.

\#

Fireflies flooded the stadium that night as the show was letting out. As if they'd all chosen to come see the cage match, too.

To hear the people of Damphry tell it, those fireflies looked less like bugs than demons, dive-bombing the populace.

\#

I thought I was supposed to win the cage match, but I was at the top—just about to hoist a leg over—when Geri caught my ankle. She stood, balanced on the top rope as it sank beneath her weight, threatening to give way. She stood balanced with her back to the cage, head between my legs. I could just barely make out the words when she said she was sorry.

She looked sorry.

In the front row, The Emperor whispered in Silly's ear.

Geri planted me with a powerbomb off the ropes, to the center of the ring.

I'd seen stars before.

Maybe I saw them that night.

But it looked like fireflies. A whole flood of them rushing in, children screaming, hell itself raining down.

SHOOTER

I thought about going home.

I drove to Minnesota instead.

I called home along the way. Dad picked up. He said Mom was sick again, but no, I shouldn't come home. Not until I was ready.

\#

I dated Danny Derkins while we both wrestled for a little Midwest indie. We made a loop of bingo halls and fairgrounds through the spring, barely making ends meet. They were the kinds of shows where the gate was lousy, and it was understood that a portion of our compensation was free food from the concession stands. Danny and I got love drunk feeding each other sweet, pink cotton candy that melted so fast you could forget you'd tasted it in the first place.

Danny was a shooter, an old school grappler who'd wrestled in high school. He'd learned the for-real holds from old-timers to choke out a fan who'd hopped the barricade or put a rookie in line if he was going too fast in the ring. Occasionally, the two of us grappled in hotel rooms, him going half-strength, half-speed to offer me a chance. Skill aside, he had a hundred pounds on me. We tangled in headlocks and body scissors until he inevitably pinned me down.

\#

It was all fun and games until we got to Camloon.

It was summer by then. County fair time. Camloon had a big one with a Ferris wheel that didn't creek when it turned and bright lights—none of the bulbs blown— lining bottles stacked for kids to chuck balls at them and the kinds of games where you slammed a mallet down to ring a bell to show how strong you were.

My opponent most of that summer was Hermione McGonagall. We were smalltime enough not to attract any sort of mainstream attention or legal action. She was a college girl who'd majored in English. The pedigree left her over-educated and ready to offer unsolicited thoughts on the *story of the match* or the *canonical implications* of a title change. The philosophy behind her gimmick— wearing a school robe and a red and yellow striped ascot, waving a wand like a Hogwarts wizard—wasn't uncommon on the roster. Tap into the ethos of something bigger to get attention and make it to the big time. Ditch the trademark infringements once she'd made it there.

The gimmick wasn't bad.

Hermione was the shits in the ring, though.

She couldn't take a hit right. She might have made a decent heel for her instinct to cower and whimper before any kind of impact, but she was supposed to be the hero to my villain. I had to keep her supported on my abdominal stretch and strike for sound—stomping my foot when I hit her with a forearm smash, slapping my thigh when I chopped her chest to mask how softly I hit her. When she was on offense, I had to cinch her arm across my throat and lean into her spinning heel kick to make any contact at all.

Still, we got to know one another the way you do when you're up against the same opponent night after night. You work out a degree of trust and figure out which annoyances you have to put aside. By the time we got to Camloon, we had a match down—not as much improvisation as I'd like, but a series of respectable spots to get us to eight minutes, bell to bell.

#

Hermione was the one who spotted the note.

The fairgrounds had a shed that housed a series of toilet closets, once painted white, now chipped, dulled, and dirtied to gray-brown. The red ink read, *July 3, no mercy. Everybody gets shot.* She found it July 1, our first night, and she gathered us all around to see it.

Hermione went to Calvin Gordy, the promoter. The head of our band of musclemen and misfits. He went to the guy who'd booked us, who went to whoever was in charge of the fair, who went to the police, who sent out an officer by nightfall. He poked around, looked at the red-ink warning. By then, the fair manager had sent a pimply faced teenage team to cordon off the area with caution tape that read *UNDER CONSTRUCTION*. The officer was short and slim—neither a bodybuilder nor the doughnut-eater we might have expected. He looked almost comical when The Blue Brothers, a tag team that worked a cop gimmick, walked by, each dwarfing the real policeman.

When Gordy addressed the lot of us after the fans had gone home—everyone stinking in the summer heat given the absence of showers at an outdoor event—he told us that the specialist deemed the threat, "not credible."

That announcement went over like a chili cheese dog fart with the windows rolled up. Questions about what determined credibility, and if everyone still had to wrestle and whether somebody would get metal detectors set up at the entrance gate.

Here was a threat hardly anyone knew had been made. Hermione asked if we would get the word out to fans.

Of course not, Gordy said. There were some rules of wrestling that were unimpeachable, and first among them was that no one did anything in an effort to get fans *not* to show up.

There might have been a lot more bitching and haggling had Danny not spoken up. He was at least as respected as Gordy, but without the baggage of being management.

"Some idiot tries to jack a wrestling show, and he's gonna catch a beating." He leaned over the ring ropes to spit outside, marking his territory. For these three nights, this land was a wrestling arena, and wrestlers claimed what they could through physicality. "Anybody tries anything on us, we take care of it," Danny said.

A quiet rumble of approval. Gordy tried echoing the sentiments in his own words—a lukewarm imitation of Danny's confidence and call to arms. The crowd dispersed, and I held Danny's hand on the way back to his pickup truck.

#

At the hotel, after we'd showered and eaten, Danny wasn't so sure.

"Somebody comes at me with his fists, with a knife even, I'll handle him. But a gun? I may not even get him in arm's reach."

I reminded him of what he'd said in the ring. "It's all of us in this together." I coiled an arm around his midsection, pulling him into bed. "We'll all be there."

"It's everybody." He stared straight ahead toward the television. We had it turned off. When we started sharing a room he'd told me he couldn't sleep without it on, and I told him I couldn't sleep with it, so we went back and forth. Whoever was up later got their way, turning it on or off after the other wouldn't notice. Except those nights when the sleeper woke, and we grappled over the remote and more often than not it tumbled to the floor. It didn't matter anyway because wrestling gave way to kissing to touching to not sleeping at all.

There was no back and forth that night. "I'm worried about everybody," he said.

\#

I dreamed of wrestling in a USO show in the middle of a combat zone. Gordy was there at ringside. I leaned through the ropes and told him this didn't seem safe. A bullet whizzed past my ear and exploded a turnbuckle. He reiterated that the threat wasn't credible.

\#

Danny wasn't the only one concerned. It may have been his vote of confidence that had swung the momentum after Gordy's announcement, but an undercurrent of fear lingered, too, amplified by a night to reflect and worry.

At the show the next day, Odin Alexander, a six-foot-ten mountain of a man with poor coordination, but the size to always ensure him a job in wrestling, told a story to anyone who'd listen. He was a junior in high school. A sophomore who got bullied at school and knocked around by his dad at home finally lost it and brought in a gun. He opened fire in the lunchroom and killed a basketball player, clipped his cheerleader girlfriend's shoulder with a shot before a social studies teacher tackled the shooter. A bunch of the other kids dogpiled him to keep him down. The gun went off again in the melee but the stray bullet only hit a water fountain.

Odin wasn't part of the pile on. Six-ten, pushing three hundred pounds he might have helped a lot in that scenario, but he'd seen himself as the biggest target in the room. He took cover under a cafeteria table, head in his hands and rocking until after it was all over. He told us it was the scariest moment of his life.

But the moral of the story wasn't what I'd expected about fear and trauma and chaos and death.

"Somebody wants to kill a bunch of people, they aren't going to announce themselves," Odin said. "That's asking for fewer targets, more security. If they mean to shoot, they'll come at you when you least expect it."

When you least expect it can mean different things to different people. Maybe it meant that prior warning was a surefire sign of a hoax, like Odin would suggest.

But maybe it meant the shooter would come a day later when everyone was heaving a sigh of relief. Or maybe the shooter'd come a day early. Not the end of our three-night stand, but the middle.

Maybe the shooter would come to the backstage tent where the wrestlers were getting ready and pick off as many of us as he could instead of going after the fans.

I tried to visualize hiding places. Not only the quickest, but the subtlest means of getting out of the glow of the spotlights trained on the ring. How effective it might be to hide under the timekeeper's table, or if there'd be room when the timekeeper, ring announcer, and front row fans inevitably took that refuge first.

I overheard two of the boys talking from ringside before the gates opened, before the inevitable trickle of early comers who'd chosen the fair for their day's entertainment specifically to see the wrestlers. They were the ones who would stake out front row seats and sit for hours to ensure their close-up look at the action and maybe get rewarded by some of us coming by to chit chat before opening bell. Wrestlers would talk openly with fans like that nowadays, not like the olden days when it was so engrained to stay in character whenever a fan might be listening. But we wouldn't talk with fans about the specter of a shooter.

We talked about it early, just us around. New York Nick Nettles pointed to a scaffold rig. "That's where a shooter would position himself. Open fire during the show from the highest point available, or maybe start shooting after the show. Pick people off while they're exiting, all single file, pushing to get in the line of fire before they realize what's happening."

"I thought the same thing, the minute I saw the set up," Justin Ovative added. The premise seemed absurd, that he'd have considered the likelihood of where a shooter would position himself before anyone knew there was a threat.

We were all looking around that day.

\#

That night, Hermione was late to catch me on a plancha to ringside during our match. I had to adjust mid-air and wound up hitting my hand hard against her shoulder, jamming my index finger.

While I iced my hand backstage, Hermione noted which finger was swelling. She speculated it was a symbol. "If you can't use your trigger finger, maybe that represents how the shooter won't be able to pull the trigger. Maybe we'll all be spared. "

My finger hurt like a bitch.

I told her to shut the fuck up.

\#

Fight or flight. If somebody had a gun and tried to hurt us, there was some small pleasure in the fantasy of that fight. I imagined getting the drop on the shooter. Some combination of happenstance, maybe distraction. I'd nail him with a flying drop kick that momentarily knocked the gun from his hands and follow up with a rear naked choke. Keep pressure on his throat until he was desperate. Keep squeezing until he passed out or was dead. Or straddle his torso and punch him with all I had.

One of the ironies of being a wrestler is that you learn to hit people without really hurting them, but you also learn to fight for real as your body hardens into callouses, and a fan gets handsy at ringside or somebody recognizes you at a bar after the show and wants to try you. It wasn't a stretch to imagine beating someone until my knuckles bled.

I might be a hero. Get some good press, maybe a key to the city. Maybe build some sort of action hero element into my wrestling gimmick. That'd be all well and good, but mostly I imagined the satisfying crunch of his nose beneath my fist.

#

Other wrestlers talked about a prospective shooting, too. Some of them about their own future heroism, tackling a gunman, clobbering him with a legit chair shot to the head. Andre Funk talked about snatching the gun from the would-be shooter and turning the tables *just to watch the little fucking shit shit himself.*

"And what'd you do after that?" Danny asked.

The response came back meeker. Something about turning him over to the police, and something about popping him one in the nose on the hand off. Nick Nettles patted his back and nodded along. "You think the police would be OK with you popping some kid in the face right in front of them?"

"Who said it's a kid?" Danny asked.

"What if it's a girl?" Nick asked.

Andre wasn't making eye contact anymore. "We'd take care of it." He looked to me. "Maybe I'd hand her over to your girlfriend to teach her a lesson."

#

When we spotted him, he was male. Pale, white, tall and lanky, wearing a black trench coat.

Nick Nettles pointed him out, but Danny was already watching the kid when he took his seat in the back row of folding chairs. Duffel bag at his side.

Word spread. We all watched him, crowded at the edge of the makeshift curtain, positioned to block the audience's view of us coming out of the tent we used for a backstage area.

The kid in the trench coat tapped on his phone with a fury.

"There might be more of them," Hermione said. "He's plotting."

"Or he's a teenager with a cell phone," I said. But no one listened. It was transparent what I was doing—the conditioning to minimize a threat, to set everyone at ease, even when there was every reason to be on high alert.

"Do we tell Gordy?" Nick asked. "Or go straight to the police?"

Danny stepped past him.

He shot past the kids in the front rows, reaching out scraps of paper for autographs, and blew past the portly guy in the third row who tried to snap a selfie with him.

Danny got to the kid in the trench coat.

Danny didn't say a word at all, but rather reached past the trench coat to snatch a hold of the kid's t-shirt, rip him up into the air, and turn him around. Danny pinned the teenager's arm back in a hammerlock, and then threaded his own arm up through the space between the kid's arm and back. Another arm slid around the kid's throat and he clasped his fingers.

Hang around wrestlers long enough and you lose sight of how big they are. Danny's fist wasn't much smaller than the kid's head. The cross-face chicken wing hold could easily dislocate the kid's shoulder, all Danny had to do was flex.

The kid was whimpering when I got there, Nick a step behind me. Here we were, living what must have been

Danny's particular daydream about a shooter. And still the question: what next?

"Check the bag, numb skulls." Danny said it through gritted teeth, not because he was applying the pressure or it was difficult to hold the kid. Because it was difficult to strike this particular balance between holding him and not really hurting him.

I unzipped the bag.

Nick pulled out the bottle of lotion. "What the hell?"

The spout was baby blue. Also in the bag: diapers, wipes, a packet of apple sauce mixed with crushed strawberry.

"Let him go," I said.

\#

Gordy got involved. There was a commotion of course, of people taking videos on their phones and the kid selling like he was half dead on the ground after Danny let him go. Next thing, the kid's mother and toddler brother were on the scene—the ones he'd come early to save seats for, while the little one watched the carousel go around one more time before the wrestling show.

\#

I read an article about false alarms. That they may not have the same catastrophic effects on a community as a shooting—not the same mourning of lost lives, not the same trauma to the survivors.

Still, once you've put yourself in the position of considering a shooting, eyeing the person standing next to you as a prospective mass murderer, reckoning with your own mortality—it's hard to come back from that.

\#

We got lucky. It wasn't just the kid in the trench coat who was curious to see a wrestling show. It was a whole family of marks who recognized half the roster by other gimmicks we'd played in other territories. The kind of family that went to a match anyplace within a few-hour drive and didn't give a second thought to bringing a toddler along because it was important to indoctrinate him early.

They agreed not to press charges against Danny or the company in exchange for the opportunity to go backstage. Gordy made sure every last one of us pose for pictures with them, last of all Danny who, at the kids request, put on the cross-face chicken wing again—not the shoot version, but rather a looser, sloppier hold than would ever pass Danny's standards in an actual wrestling ring.

\#

A lot of us stuck around the extra night after our last show in Camloon. We had a week before our next spot, no rush to get out of town, and the fair was having a fireworks display.

We didn't want to pay to get in, but that's one of the nice things about pyrotechnics, as opposed to wrestling. You don't need to get up close. You can watch what happens from the parking lot.

It wasn't all that impressive of a show, but I'd always found something romantic about fireworks and held hands with Danny when they started going off. Our bodies both went rigid before long, though.

The reality settled in that the explosions sounded an awful lot like gun shots.

If you were in a certain state of mind, the red embers falling from the sky could look an awful lot like blood.

The two of us left before the fireworks were over.

\#

I didn't stay in the Midwest long. They had the kind of territory where the roster ballooned in the summer months with so many opportunities to perform and then shrank back down when temperatures cooled and fair season was over.

Danny and I said our goodbyes. It was understood we weren't in it for the long haul, no point in kidding ourselves about long distance. That was for rookies and dreamers.

The word about the shooting threat spread—a story that made the rounds here and there through other territories.

I heard through the grapevine that that warning on the shed hadn't been new. It had been there at least three years earlier, according to Big Poppa Cool, who said he and the boys had told Gordy about it then and gotten brushed off.

I was angry.

But that next summer, Danny worked the fairs again. He sent me a picture of where the warning still stood, the red ink bright against the white shed, as if someone had stenciled over it in a fresh coat to keep the threat alive.

I texted him back to tell him what I'd heard from Big Poppa Cool, and to ask if they talked to the police again, or at least the man who managed the fairgrounds. They couldn't let a threat like that sit there forever, could they?

STOLEN

Years passed. Mom died.

I went back for the funeral, back for the first time since I'd hit the road. I was in the midst of a feud with Susy Hamilton, deep in the heart of Texas. I flew back to Syracuse—a luxury that blew through my meager savings.

An aunt—my mother's sister—picked me up from the airport. She put a hand over the big bruise on the right side of my face. "You having boyfriend troubles?"

Mom never told people I was a wrestler, only that I'd left home for work. I suppose every encounter with extended family is disorienting. All the more so when so many people are drawn together. Compound that with a return to the old house. If Mom were still alive—if there were another reason for bringing this collection of people together that would have also made me return home—she would have cleaned with a fury. She wasn't a dedicated homemaker in the day to day, but she was conscious enough of her image to keep her car meticulously clean for the sort of run-ins that inevitably come up in a small town. She delegated cleaning tasks to me and to Dad whenever we were going to host company, and I learned from watching Dad that I need only wait a few hours without doing them before Mom would tend to washing the windows and vacuuming the floor herself.

At the wake, paper plates and Solo cups found space amidst the clutter of unsorted mail, dusty old watches and paperweights and ceramic cat figurines, there was a sink full of dirty dishes and fuzzy black funk spotted the toilet.

Dad wore the suit he'd put on for the funeral, but otherwise made himself at home, regardless of company, relaxed on his recliner, television on even if no one could hear it.

In my wrestling life, there was always something to be done. Work out, travel to the next town, get to the arena in time for the run-through, wrestle, shower, get to the bar, get some shut-eye, do it all again.

At home—at what I'd come to know more squarely, more accurately as my father's house—everything was slower. Even when Dad fell asleep on the recliner altogether, only some of the visitors took the hint to leave. Uncle Charlie slipped the remote from Dad's armrest and put on a baseball game, and made idle chit-chat about how that goddamn moneyball crap ruined the game. Some of the women made gestures toward cleaning, straightening photo frames, collecting crumpled napkins from the mantle. from My great-aunt Maude asked how Massachusetts was a third or fourth time, until I stopped correcting her and told her years outdated stories of taking shelter from snowstorms and how Boston really was a walking city and how the lobster was better, but too expensive to eat much.

"You keep working," she said. "You're still young. You'll make money. Just keep working."

#

I drove back to Texas. Dad insisted I take Mom's car—it was paid off and he said she'd want me to have a more reliable car. He was right. I could imagine Mom handing me the keys herself. Knowing it was right. Cringing with the knowledge I wouldn't keep up on oil changes as often as I should and would keep driving until the low fuel light came on.

#

Rich Stewart Jr. came back from the wrestling ring to the locker room all jacked up, clapping his hands, spraying sweat and spittle. "That's how you steal the show!" he told anyone who'd listen.

I was mostly working curtain-jerker matches with Susy those days, a rock solid worker whose career had looked up those months when she was dating Rich, the boss's son, and whose prospects had stagnated after they split up, or as Susy described it, when Rich moved on to his next flavor of the week, a British crumpet who wrestled under the name Lady London.

Susy clarified her point of view: Rich *never* stole the show, both because his matches were rarely good and because it was impossible to steal the show from a main event spot. The show already belonged to people working on top.

Still Rich held up his hand for high fives and slapped it on the backs of the boys who didn't bother to acknowledge him. He breezed past the girls, straight to Lady London to scoop her up in his arms and kiss her, open-mouthed and sloppy.

Susy said that was high school QB 101. Ignore the girls to make them want you. The strategy had worked in duping her, she admitted, when she first got to Ring Master Promotions. (Also, yes, senior year, Rich really was his private school's starting quarterback.)

For as loud as Rich was, he couldn't compel the attention of the locker room that particular evening for long. Tele Daddy—a three hundred-pound Samoan who claimed lineage with the sprawling Anoa'i wrestling family that included The Rock—threw down his gym bag. He held court in the center of the locker room as even Rich himself shut up to listen. Daddy asked, "Who stole from me?"

He pinched his leather wallet between his massive thumb and forefinger. He'd had three hundred-seventeen dollars cash in his wallet and only two hundred-sixty-seven of it was still there. Nobody was leaving the locker room until he got his money back.

Rich was the first to speak, holding up his hands. "Big man, big man." He called a lot of the boys by *big man* or *little man*, corresponding to whether they were objectively bigger or smaller than him. "Can you possibly tell me you know exactly how much cash you had?"

Tele Daddy didn't back down. "I know my money."

Rich quizzed him on whether he might have bought a soda when he got to the arena, and if in so doing, a bill or two might have fallen out of his wallet? Or did he pay cash when he gassed up the van he compulsively drove from town to town, shuttling his friends, blasting hair metal.

Tele Daddy repeated that he knew his money. He proceeded to go make the rounds one by one, eye to eye, to ask if we knew anything about his missing cash. I smelled hamburger on his breath, Old Spice from his body. He slathered it on after his showers, a responsible big man, conscious of how easily a big body could stink.

I told him I didn't know anything.

It wasn't the kind of locker room where everybody stuck around through the last match, so there was no way to conduct a full investigation. By the end of Tele Daddy's questioning—after Rich himself had said he didn't know anything—Rich shifted tacks from skeptic to crusader. Maybe moved by Tele Daddy's conviction. Maybe something else.

"We don't steal from one another," Rich said. "That's wrestler code. And if we figure out who did this, you can rest assured they'll get theirs."

It rung hollow. Like the kind of promo where the wrestler was reading lines someone wrote for him rather than speaking from the heart.

Tele Daddy watched and listened.

\#

I stole a few times. I don't trust anyone who says they haven't. The differences come in regard to what or how much you stole, or from whom, or at what point in life.

For me, it was CDs from Chart Toppers, back when they were a thing in the 1990s, peddling new music at fifteen-to-twenty dollars a disc. I didn't take the new music, though, saddled with big plastic cases with their anti-theft devices. I focused instead on the bargain bin. My pulse pounded that first time, looking around, sliding the CD under the cover of my jacket and walking with my hand pinned to it, equal parts to keep it from slipping free and so I could act like I was merely carrying it if anyone asked me what I was doing. A feeble lie, sure. But if I stuck to it, how could they prove I was lying and was it worth pressing a teenage girl over a $5.99 CD?

I got away with it.

Then it became a habit.

I didn't stop until I got caught.

There was a lesson in that moment when the two store employees in their neon green polos closed in on me before I got to the exit and told me to open my jacket. It wasn't any one mistake that revealed me, but my bad habit of coming to the store multiple times in the same day, sifting through the bargain bin and leaving. Never buying anything. One of the employees—a teenage boy with bad acne—relayed to the other—a woman I took to be college-aged and some sort of manager—that I was *the one I was telling you about.*

I got off easy. A stern talking to from a mall cop and a warning not to set foot in Chart Toppers again. My life went on.

\#

Susy was the first to vocalize what I was thinking— what it turned out half the locker room had in mind.

Rich was the thief.

There was an absurdity to the theory. RMP was one of the big indies—one of the best-paying promotions shy of the truly national wrestling companies with cable TV deals. The wrestler's life wasn't lucrative, but working for RMP, if you were smart about sharing hotel rooms, ferreting away a day's worth of Danishes and fruit from the continental breakfast, and packing people into cars to split the tab on gas—if you were creatively frugal, then you made enough to save up for a rainy day. Tele Daddy even led a crew of wrestlers with Roth IRAs.

Out of everyone, you'd think Rich would have the least to worry about, the boss's son and booked on top—a spot that meant more than a spotlight, but inevitably a bigger percentage of gates, probably a bigger base salary, too, not to mention that the merchandise tables pedaled t-shirts and posters with his likeness on them and he collected royalties.

But Rich hadn't always worked for his dad.

He had a brief spell in WWE's developmental system, which the boys tended to dismiss as more a favor to his old man than a demonstration of his potential. He promptly blew that chance on the first random drug test. He'd spent a spell in Smoke City after that for a change in scenery, a chance to reset. It was a respectable enough place to work, more or less on par with RMP if only because the wrestlers got put up in a casino hotel and didn't have to travel much, instead focusing their efforts on five-nights-a-week shows.

The word was murky about if Rich left Smoke City because his gambling debt was out of control and he was worried about getting his legs broken, or if his father had bailed him out of trouble, or if he'd been banned from one of the gaming floors for a card-counting scheme. Maybe none of the stories were on point. Maybe they all were. Hear a story from a wrestler, and there're always shades of gray.

Away from the bad influences of Smoke City he still had his tendencies. He instigated poker games among the boys in the locker room and found his way to off-track betting sites whenever there was one in striking distance of the arena.

Susy told me when they dated, she'd spotted him a hundred dollars once. It was against her principles to loan money to a boyfriend or a co-worker, but he came to her wide-eyed and desperate. "Like he'd seen a ghost." We watched him talking on the other side of the locker room. Susy stretched athletic tape, coiling it tight around her wrist. "Like the devil himself was after him."

#

The boys told stories. A lot of them included something getting stolen.

They told these stories casually, apropos nothing, old timers spinning yarns and younger talents trying to get a word in edgewise for a tall tale.

Big Bruiser Olsen, a bald super heavyweight with a hairy back, said he organized a small-time show and ordered five hundred flyers from a local print shop. The place messed up the order and only made fifty copies, nowhere near enough to paper the town.

"This tampon-necked geek behind the counter has the nerve to tell me there's no time to print more because they're busy." Bruiser ate from a plate of spaghetti. RMP offered catering, which was a leg up from a lot of smaller companies, but the wrestlers had a tendency to complain about it always being cheap food loaded with carbs, like pasta or bologna and American cheese sandwich spreads. Bruiser was never cut like a body builder, never counted calories. He was old school enough not to buck if he had free food in front of him. "So, after hours, me and the boys go back to that copy shop."

Bruiser said they were prepared to bust a window, only to find that whoever had closed up for the night forgot to lock up. Maybe they figured they didn't have anything anybody would want to steal—little of value besides the copy machines themselves and who was going to move three hundred-plus pounds of metal and plastic?

By the time Bruiser and his friends had gotten the machine back to the hotel room they used as a makeshift office and wrangled it through the doorframe (they had to take off the door and still knocked off some auxiliary pieces), their priorities had shifted. The original plan was to run off the extra flyers they were owed, but with the print shop being unlocked like it was, no sign that any alarms had been triggered, they decided they'd return to the scene of the crime and wallpaper it with five hundred or so photo copies of Bruiser's ass.

The machine buckled under his weight, but did successfully churn out copies—a hundred or so before they blew a fuse. They never did get around to hanging up the copies. Instead, Bruiser remembered getting drunk in the dark, nobody able to keep track of how many beers they'd drank individually, though, between the five of them, they'd railroaded through two cases.

I asked Bruiser what happened to the copy machine.

He shook his head, smiling with wonder. "Damned if I can remember."

#

When word got around that we hadn't sold more than fifty tickets for a show outside Philly, some of the boys went to Rich Senior. Would we bother putting on the show with a house that small? Were we pricing ourselves out of the market? Bruiser, older, fearless, more secure in his spot, asked the question more directly: *how long can we keep pushing your kid on top when he wouldn't draw maggots to rotten hamburger?*

Rich's dad told anyone who'd listen that it was a walk-up town, which in the parlance of the business meant people would show up before bell time, cash in hand, and fill up the seats.

Bruiser muttered that it'd never been a walk-up town before.

We worked in front of maybe a hundred people out of the thousand folding chairs set up in the arena. Susy insisted on a safer, quieter version of the match we'd been developing, ditching her plancha spot and the super-brain buster she'd been perfecting. I still went for my crash-and-burn missed corkscrew moonsault to set up the hero for the finish—despite her insistence I go for a simpler splash instead. I'd had it instilled in me when I worked smaller time promotions to give fans their money's worth, no matter how few of them there were.

Rich went forty minutes in a main event of mostly chin locks and laying on the mat breathing heavily to sell the lowkey offense. The few fans who were left started clearing our early.

You'd think that his dad might address the issue then, either in a closed-door conversation with Rich or some public declaration to apologize to the roster. He could've at least offered some explanation as to why he was staying the course.

But as I was coming to understand in RMP, it was never that straightforward when it came to Rich and his dad. After the generic praise for a good show, the old man singled out my match with Susy as an example of what he didn't want to see. "You win back a town when you go all out for it. You lose it altogether when you half ass it."

Susy and I both knew better than to say anything. I could even bear to nod along. Susy kept her eyes fixed down on the cement floor. If I weren't sitting right beside her, I might not have noticed that slight tremor in her body, pulsing with indignation.

Rich Senior went on to announce a show in Duggan, a bigger market and a town where RMP had a history of drawing well. The event would feature the King and Queen of the Road tournaments, for which a car dealership he was connected with had agreed to donate new cars to be awarded to the winners.

I noticed one of the boys perk up, revealing himself a rookie, hopeful he might be the chosen one and drive off with some new wheels. One of the first rules you learn in wrestling, though, is it's not just the storylines and who wins and loses that are works of fiction, but any prizes, too, any sense of prestige attached to an accomplishment.

No one was driving off with one of those cars.

Rich Senior followed up. "We're going to gimmick the windshields with sugar glass so they shatter when somebody hits them. Junior and Dark Warrior are going to do a big spot, and we've got not one, but two cars so there's a backup."

Richie clapped his hands. "This is going to be big business!"

No one joined him in celebrating.

His father went on with the last item of business while the roster was all there. "It's come to my attention there was another theft tonight, of Gary Page's watch."

Gary was an old timer. Classy. A friend of Rich Senior doing a short tour with us as a favor to a chum from back in the day. He was old enough for it to be believable he'd have a nice watch. Old school enough to go straight to Rich Senior to complain rather than making a scene in front of the boys.

Rich Senior went on about doing the right thing and folks saying something if they'd seen anything. I ventured a look around the room to vacant stares and nods. To Tele Daddy, cracking his knuckles in the corner.

\#

Over beers, after a show, Susy told me how she stole her way into the business.

She started on the up and up. Told her folks, a week before she would've started college that she wasn't going. She told them she needed to wrestle.

I could relate to that impulse.

Technically, it wasn't stealing when she walked to the bank and withdrew five thousand dollars cash from the fund her folks had scrounged together. It was a joint account; the money was in her name.

Still, she knew what the money was meant for, and that didn't have anything to do with hitchhiking to the training camp an old wrestler named Delilah LeRoux ran across state lines, or Susy buying her first pair of wrestling boots.

I asked her if she'd ever spoken to her parents since.

"Of course," she said. "It was rocky for a few months, but after I'd started wrestling and paying my own way, what were they going to do?" A waitress delivered our sampler platter, all onion rings and buffalo wings and potato skins smothered in melted cheese, dotted with bacon and chives. A splurge, but the bar sold half-price appetizers after eleven p.m. and we were starving. "Mom still needles me about the money sometimes, though. She says I owe her."

I bit into the first wing, spicier than I expected, but once my teeth had sunk through the flesh, it was too late to turn back. The fried skin all stuck together, leaving little choice but to tear it all off the bone in that first bite, my chapped lips burning with the heat.

"She says I stole the money," Susy said. "One time I told her that's how I felt about all the college plans they she and Dad made for me—that they were trying to steal my life."

#

Rich got caught red-handed going through Billy Glover's duffel bag in a broom closet. From what I could glean, it sounded like it was some sort of set up, where he'd acted protective over the bag like he had something valuable inside, then acted too distracted in conversation to remember to put a combination lock on his locker, all to entice the thief into going for it.

Tiny Terror, one of the little-people wrestlers, played look out. It wasn't enough for Rich to open the locker or even to take out the bag—that could have been explained away. The key was for him to leave the locker room with it and sequester himself away. The guys surrounded Rich. Tele Daddy stood over him, arms crossed, every bit the enforcer he played in the ring. And Rich laughed.

"Guys, it was a rib! You really think I'm going to steal from the boys and hide to rifle through your things? I figured this'd break the ice about all the thefts going around. It's a joke."

He couldn't explain the punchline, though—what he was going to do with the bag or its contents, or when he would've given it back.

Rich Senior asked what was going on. He heard out the prosecution and he heard his son's excuses, feebler in front of his father, when it was clear no one from the locker room believed his lies.

#

I got mugged once. Weeks out of training camp, still new to the road, driving the same beatup Chevy sedan I'd commuted to high school with in another life.

I was getting in the car, no one else in sight, when the guy came up to me, navy ski mask, switchblade gleaming in the streetlight, and demanded my phone and wallet.

I gave him what he asked for.

He rifled through the wallet, right there in front of me, clearly disappointed that I only had three dollars cash. I almost apologized to him. I told the other wrestlers about it by way of warning, as if this might be some pandemic they ought to be wary of.

Iceberg Jones laughed in my face. "He must have been out of his damn mind."

Other wrestlers laughed, too. Because wrestlers were strong and used to getting hit. Because knife or not, most wrestlers would have taken their chances on a fight.

Sandy Jensen asked why I didn't scream. The other wrestlers were nearby. Someone would've heard.

All I could say was that it hadn't occurred to me to call for help or to fight back.

It was a long time ago.

#

When I made my entrance through the curtain for the show in Duggan, I walked right by the twin sedans, shining under a fresh coat of wax. I gave one an extra look—I could pass it off as lusting after the car, because after all my match with Susan was a quarterfinal bout for the Queen of the Road tournament, one of these automobiles the prize.

I looked for signs of the sugar glass that would shatter with ease beneath the weight of a body, but whoever had gimmicked it had done a good enough job that it was tough to tell.

Susy and I had started the conversation backstage, born from a shared dissatisfaction at our place on the card. Lady London would win the women's tournament and pose for photos with the car earmarked for her—photos that would circulate in RMP promotional materials. The car a further establishment of RMP's legitimacy—that while other minor league companies couldn't afford real leather for their championship belts, we had vehicles at our disposal. Lady London's victory would also fast track her status as a title contender.

I'd beat Susy, then get beaten by Canadian Queen, who'd lose to Lady London in the finals. As such, me vs. Susy was set up to be forgotten. No one remembers a match that's only there to feed the bracket, a route for the losing finalist to get to the end of the night.

When Susy I talked, we mused about stealing the show anyway. About what it might take to stage something that would get fans talking, even after we were both eliminated from the tournament.

What if we didn't have restrictions?

What if there were no consequences?

In another backstage conversation, Tele Daddy gave his notice. He was leaving the company after this show. His contract had run up a month before and he'd been working on a handshake deal, as a nicety. But a guy like him had no shortage of places to go, and there weren't many places where anyone had to worry about hiding their valuables from a thief who was the booker's son.

I didn't have a long-term contract, working shot-to-shot, with the implication that if they stayed happy with me, I'd stay employed. Susy was signed, but only for a month longer.

What if—

\#

Tele Daddy told a story about getting in a brawl with a bunch of firefighters. Young. Strong. Brave. Far from pushovers, but they weren't wrestlers.

It was a parking lot brawl—outside a bar of course—where somebody from one side beat somebody from the other in a twenty-dollar game of billiards, and insults emerged about how wrestlers were phonies and weren't so tough.

The fight took a little time, but the wrestlers got the better of it. Cooler heads prevailed when they heard police sirens. No matter if the wrestlers were in the right—who knew if they were?—no way small town police were going to side with them over local fire fighters. The wrestlers knew they were screwed, because even if they could take the cops there was no good ending to that scenario, only arrests or somebody getting shot. No, the best thing to do was to run.

But how to get away?

And wouldn't they get caught anyway?

Tele Daddy was just a kid, cutting his teeth in wrestling then, and it was his uncle who hollered the idea to steal the fire engine. It was an obviously terrible idea, but who was Tele Daddy to argue? He jumped in with other boys in the cabin, others hanging off the side as his uncle turned on the siren and they tore through the night.

"You stole a fire truck?" one of the young boys asked, not because the story was ambiguous, or even out of incredulity, but with the sheer wonder of a child hearing something sensational.

Tele Daddy nodded. "Those were wild times."

\#

Susy and I worked the match we wanted to.

We didn't start with a lock up and chain wrestle. We traded haymakers.

We didn't save energy for the next round the way the veterans would have advised for any first-round-of-a-tournament match, or set the bar low this early in the card, so it wouldn't be so hard for bigger names to follow.

I hit a top rope hurricanrana on Susy.

She kicked out at one, hit a round house kick, and set me up for a burning hammer.

The ref cautioned us to settle down. I shoved him out of the way and swept the ring bell, house mic, and a pitcher of water from the timekeeper's table, so I could slam Susy's body down on it.

The ref called for a double count out, signaling we were out of the ring too long, scrapping the match because there was no point in prolonging a match that wasn't going to follow the script.

We kept fighting.

Officials tried to separate us. Here's an insider secret: if you've got two people who know how to fight, they'll find a way to keep fighting. You know the fix is in when they let a couple white collars keep them apart before they get another shot in.

Me and Susy could fight.

We fought the white shirts. She muttered, *come get me*, a signal that her heel character was going to run and that I should chase her. We knew we were faster than the people out there to split us apart. Put some distance between us and them, and we could keep fighting.

We fought at the cars.

Susy poked me in the eye and then pulled my hair until she'd wrangled me up onto the roof of the car.

She hit a piledriver through the windshield.

No need for a backup car. The first worked like a charm, glass shattering on impact with my skull.

I bled, but it didn't hurt much.

Maybe that was the adrenaline talking.

The real paramedics came out to extract my limp body, and I imagined the pandemonium in the locker room, management and the boys watching on a monitor. Was this a real fight? Had Susy really meant to hurt me?

She stood on the hood of the other, pristine car. She was triumphant.

And just as my back made contact with the stretcher, I sprung to life.

I tackled her. Susy's back hit the glass first, technically, but my skull was only a half-beat behind, exploding it.

Our skin shredded, the second car wrecked, we waited for the medical crew.

\#

It's so easy to steal something. It's not just the cold-hearted criminal who does it, but the average teen, the wrestler after a couple too many drinks.

My first real gig in wrestling, back in New England, I stole somebody's boyfriend.

I never did pay the price properly from the other woman, but I worked a spot show in New Mexico years later, and one of her friends knew who I was before I knew who she was and she spat in my face.

And that's the thing about a certain kind of stealing. You know you were in the wrong. You get caught. You pay the consequences. You never get rid of that warm heat of shame on your skin.

I let that wad of phlegm run its course, dripping off my cheek like I deserved it.

\#

In an ordinary, functional locker room, Susy and I'd have been greeted with cold stares and a veteran or two telling us what damn fools we were for going into business for ourselves before management told us we were fired.

We came back to a standing ovation.

Applause loud enough we could barely hear Richie's complaint, for as loud as I'm sure he was yelling it.

You stole my spot! You stole my spot!

I draped my bloody arm over Susy's war-torn shoulder and touched the top of my head to the side of hers. "No," I said. "We stole the show."

SMOKE CITY

I didn't tell my father when I moved on to Smoke City.

Madeleine cradled my ankles in her armpits, my body bent into a crescent, legs long and oiled, feet bare in the customs of Smoke City Wrestling. I moaned the way she'd told me to backstage. A sound of pain that could as easily be mistaken for a sex noise because that's what the men had come to hear.

I understood in that moment how wrestling might be made sexy. The two of us wore booty shorts and sports bras, skin shining, athletic bodies pushing and pulling against one another.

I felt my ankle slip loose. My leg crashed to the mat. The hold hadn't hurt, but the fall did a little. Madeleine crouched into a half crab, some semblance of a grappling transition, like I'd fought partially free but she nonetheless still had me, all the while positioning my body to be more comfortable, less prone to actually getting hurt.

Madeleine was a safe worker. She'd been wrestling in Smoke City for five years and prided herself on knowing this variation on professional wrestling as well as anyone.

We sold sex to the men who drove in to Smoke City— a casino town—for card games and booze and to see what other trouble they might get into over long weekends. I came to the territory on the premise of good pay days, no travel, little of the wear and tear that comes with full-impact matches. Other girls reassured me if I could check my dignity at the door, it was a good place to cool my jets for a year or two and pad my bank account, add years to my career from giving my back a break from powerbombs and spine busters in favor of sexy looking holds.

My first night in, I wasn't so sure.

I won, but it didn't mean anything—even less than the typical predetermined outcome of a professional match. Madeleine had been up front that most of us would take turns winning and losing, and the only exceptions were the girls with resting bitch face who worked better in dominating roles and girls like Lucy—a real girl-next-door type who sold better than anyone, so men would clamor to hear her whimpers escalate over the course of a match until the climax, screaming her submission.

I picked up the duke with a figure four leg lock that saw Madeleine shriek, stretching out her long neck in a way that drew a roar from the crowd. She ravaged fistfuls of hair and cast her tearful desperation at one man in the front row before screaming, "I give up! Please stop hurting me!"

I didn't love that type of submission—the kind reserved for only the most cowardly jobber in most wrestling territories. I'd learn that was the nature of Smoke City Wrestling for the loser to be rendered a trembling, inconsolable mess whom the men in the crowd might fantasize about massaging the sore body of. I didn't love what I had to do either, standing over her body, biceps flexed, a foot on her heaving bosom. They called it a victory pose, inviting flash photographs.

"Isn't it all kind of voyeuristic?" I asked Madeleine in the locker room.

She smirked. "It's wrestling."

I'd shared a locker room with Dragon Princess when she'd talked about how it was a nobler pursuit to use physicality to entertain the masses by pretending to hurt someone rather than really hurting someone. I'd heard Pit Bull Peters talk about offering entertainment that transcended language—a narrative men like his Polish immigrant father could understand fresh off the boat, before he picked up the English language. I, myself, had mused wrestling storytelling might help us all better understand the human condition.

Madeleine was less idealistic than all that. Pragmatic. She'd come to Smoke City as a trapeze artist, flying high in a niche circus show at one of the casinos until a torn rotator cuff and resulting complications meant she couldn't perform safely anymore. She was in the habit of eating well and maintaining the musculature necessary to swing across high beams, and parlayed all of that to her wrestling career, such as it was—safer in this world of make-believe combat. "Men came to the circus to stare at our bodies, too," she said. "When we wrestle, we don't bother pretending they're here to see anything else."

The men came to us for a novelty, maybe a fetish, a step removed from the burlesque shows or strip clubs all over Smoke City. But for some men, watching wasn't enough. Some men wanted in on the action.

In the locker room shower, Madeleine explained, "Sessions are where the real money's at here." She said men booked private sessions in casino hotel rooms to stage matches of their own with girls from Smoke City Wrestling. Some came with elaborate scripts and scenarios. The girl was a petty thief caught stealing in the room and needed some discipline. Or she was a government interrogator, the guy a terrorist she set to squeeze between her thighs until he confessed his secrets. A lot of men didn't want such pretense at all, though. They wanted to wrestle a pretty girl who knew how to apply holds and who wouldn't make him feel weird about it. So, they'd wrestle, nothing predetermined or planned besides some agreement about going half speed or to not mess with a guy's trick knee.

"Most guys who go in for this sort of thing are the submissive type," Madeleine said. "And we can ask for a premium rate for the ones who aren't. You always want another girl in the room for those ones. I bring an escort regardless—a lot of the girls do if it's not a regular customer. Nico works out all the particulars with the client, and all the money stuff. Most of us don't communicate with the client until we're in the room, unless you're like Lucy."

I learned that, in contrast to the helpless victim she'd play for the arena crowds, Lucy had a reputation for taking an active role in her bookings—messaging with clients about wardrobe choices and favorite holds and other nuances of sessions for days leading up to a meet up.

I told Madeleine I'd come to Smoke City to be a wrestler, not a prostitute.

Madeleine laughed and made the obvious joke that there wasn't much difference, but when I didn't laugh in return, she clarified that there was no sex. "I'm not going to say no girl has ever gone into business for herself and worked out something in the room, but it's not the standard. I've never done it. Nico's good about protecting us on that—making it explicit that prostitution is illegal and that's not what we're selling."

I hadn't interacted much with Nico yet. He was one of the management guys, who came across as something like a gopher, running a new microphone out to the ring when the one the ring announcer was using died during the show, and updating me and Madeleine when they mixed up the order of the matches and we wound up going on earlier. I could see a guy like that running in between girls and clients, too, though. Calm and practical, equal parts setting customers straight that wrestling didn't entitle them to anything they might want and reassuring them, too, that they really weren't getting into anything illegal.

"Sometimes a guy will get too excited and cream himself," Madeleine said. "It's an occupational hazard. And, if you want, it's grounds to call the session then and there, no refunds."

#

I asked around. When you bounce between territories you learn quickly that you can't trust what everyone says, Wrestlers are liars with their own self interests at stake, sure, but also, everyone sees the world differently, and especially if you get paid to get hit in the head night in and night out, there's every possibility you're not taking in the world through the clearest eyes.

Maybe Madeleine and Lucy worked sessions, but that didn't have to mean it was the norm. Maybe they had a reputation as whores or for lusting after money to the extent they'd do anything. But then Nico invited me out for a bite after the show. His treat.

We ate at Cardiac's, a hospital-themed burger joint a few doors down from the casino where I wrestled and stayed. The place served quarter-pound, half-pound, and full-pound patties, besides *The Coronary Embolism*, featuring two one-pound patties stacked one atop the other, dressed up with a dozen strips of bacon. An advertisement by the door proclaimed that customers ate free and got their names on a plaque if they finished that one. Cardiac's other central gimmick was that anybody who didn't clean his plate got a wooden-paddle spanking from his waitress. As we came in, one of those waitresses—in a grease-stained nurse's uniform with a low-cut top, a short skirt—thwacked away at a gleeful middle-aged customer I could only assume didn't finish his dinner on purpose.

I ordered a water and a quarter-pound burger with no bun. Nico was confident enough to get himself a half-pounder and a strawberry milkshake.

He gave a Cliff Notes version of what Madeleine had said about session wrestling. More brass tacks about how the going rate for most girls was a hundred dollars per half hour, and the rate doubled for sessions over an hour long. The girls kicked back twenty-five percent of the take to Smoke City Wrestling for facilitating the arrangements, twenty dollars an hour to Nico if we wanted him to sit in the room for safety purposes, or to film (at an extra hundred dollars an hour at the customer's expense). He conceded that most of the girls provided each other's backup or camera services and worked out for themselves what money would change hands or if they'd simply owe one another favors.

Nico went over all of this and told me that I had my first request. "Not one of the regulars. A tourist. He saw you tonight and he wants to meet up Saturday in his room if you're up for it."

Nico came across less like a pimp than an accountant, or the kind of attorney who didn't go up in front of court rooms, but rather pored over tax law and advised clients on what to pay or plea or fight or get ready for jail time.

Case in point, he told me if I didn't want to work a session, I didn't have to. "I know this is different from what you're used to. You're a serious wrestler. I saw your work from Damphry and I pushed to sign you. We need more women who can actually wrestle here in Smoke City to keep the rest of them safe."

I hadn't realized that anyone affiliated with Smoke City watched any other wrestling, besides looking for pretty girls with a cursory bonus if they knew a short arm scissors from a headlock.

The food arrived, mine a slab of greasy meat I wasn't shy about tearing into with my fingers.

Nico cut through his bun, through his burger, through all the fixings with a knife and fork, keeping his hands clean. "I'm grateful you'd come to work with us at all, so don't feel like you have to do something you aren't comfortable with. You probably do want to consider sessions, though. You'll wind up making a lot more money here than Damphry if you do." Nico paused to squeeze and jostle the plastic ketchup bottle. Nothing came. "Where's that waitress?"

I signaled over his shoulder. As if on cue, to answer Nico's question, she slapped her wooden paddle hard against a guy's backside. A young guy, maybe a college student, with a table full of hooting friends. He winced on contact red in the face, before his lips gave way to a smile.

\#

I slept on it. One of the perks of working Smoke City was getting to take up residence in a room in the casino hotel—no need to pay rent or split the fees on rooms, no next town to race to. We worked the same arena in the same casino, working largely the same matches over and over. We didn't make any real effort to keep kayfabe—the suggestion that our matches were legitimate fights. The people who came to see us were either out of towners who'd only watch us once, without a storyline to follow week in and week out, or else the local pervs who didn't make any bones about coming over and over again for the purpose of seeing the same thing.

I slept on sheets that smelled of bleach, which at least signaled they were clean, over carpet that reeked of cigarettes despite the no smoking sign posted outside the door. I mindlessly flipped through cable TV stations, imagining what it might mean to tangle limbs and stretch and scream with a man who'd paid to touch me in a room not unlike this one. I thought about it until my eyes were heavy and I dreamed about it, too. In my dreams, the man was portly and balding. The kind of man with disposable income, who didn't have much of a sex life, chronically single or else locked in a loveless marriage, all too eager to feel something. And if he touched himself alone in his hotel room, remembering the highlights from my match with Madeleine, was it so much worse to come to his room myself to reenact camel clutchess and body scissors? If it would be someone else in my place—maybe Madeleine herself—doing exactly the same thing if I said no, was there any difference at all? Any difference besides whether I had a couple hundred extra dollars?

All that, and maybe it would be a good thing to rip off the Band-Aid, get my first session over with.

\#

I told Nico I'd do it. Madeleine was standing by when I did and volunteered that she'd be the extra body in the room to make sure I was comfortable.

I was honest when I told her I couldn't imagine anything less comfortable than having another person watching. Because weren't we selling intimacy of a kind? And even if the customer was the one who wanted intimacy, would it really be more comfortable in that hotel room for my first session, the full knowledge that another, more experienced woman was looking on, judging what I did or did not do, what boundaries I did or did not erect, whether I was truly giving the customer his money's worth relative to her own standards?

She didn't fight me on it. Later, though, she lent me her Taser.

I told her I didn't think that'd be necessary.

"You'll be alone in a hotel room with a stranger who's paying to fight you."

I didn't think of it as fighting, but then, hadn't Madeleine told me some men liked to be dominated, and others like to dominate? That some men wanted to compete, even if only in a playful way to test their strength against a woman's and feel the mutual sweat and strain. They'd said some men liked to get slapped around, and how easy it might it be to cross a line. Hit him too hard and he hits back. Try to leave when time is up, but he hasn't had enough.

I took the Taser.

#

His name was John. Maybe a pseudonym. I came wearing a t-shirt and jeans over the same attire I wore to the ring. He answered the door in a white t-shirt, gym shorts, and flip flops, the comforter from the bed and a series of bath towels all laid out across the floor. He had light brown hair and was clean shaven, maybe six inches taller than me. The kind of build that suggested he might have run casually but wasn't a regular in the weight room.

Average. And young. Maybe in his mid-twenties. He thanked me for coming.

He told me it was his first time and asked how people usually started these things.

I almost told him it was my first time, too. But wasn't it part of the game to come across as confident? A warrior relative to this everyday man?

Besides which, maybe we didn't have to get to the wrestling right away.

I told him I liked to talk first, reassured him the time wouldn't count against the hour he'd booked. He sat down on a corner of the bed and, I started to sit on a far corner, then thought better of starting on the bed, and sat instead on the corner of the desk, a couple inches higher than him.

I asked him why he'd booked a session.

He blushed, and I thought maybe I'd gotten it wrong. After all, even if paying to wrestle a woman weren't illegal it still wasn't something most men would be proud about. Maybe a man more sure of himself could pick up a girl at a bar and coax her into playing out these fantasies. I was about to tell him he didn't have to answer, when he started in.

"I always imagined girls wrestling. It started when I was middle school and watched wrestling on TV, and I think my brain got confused with all the bodies grinding against each other and stuff. I started imagining girls from school and started imagining them wrestling me before I realized that any of it was sexual. Then you start putting the pieces together, like when you touch yourself that you're—" He trailed off, shy again.

"That you're masturbating," I said for him. Because isn't it easier to say words like that after someone else has said them first, like it's easier to tell someone you love them after you know they're feeling the same way?

John seemed relieved I'd said it. He told me about humping his teddy bear when he was a kid, and turning to his hand for better control, so the telltale squeaks of the bedsprings against a man-sized body wouldn't clue in his parents or his college roommate to what he was doing.

"I came here alone," he said at last. "Because I'd read about sessions and that they did them in Smoke City. And then I saw you."

This was another side of Smoke City. Not a boys' weekend full of cocktails and cigars over the craps table and getting talked into bottle service at the strip club. This was a man who had the means coming with a purpose, standing on the cusp of something. This was a lonely man. A man I could understand. A man whom I didn't think was sure he wanted to go through with wrestling a woman in a hotel room.

"You look a lot like this girl I had a crush on in high school. Betty. I never had the guts to ask her out, then she met a guy in college, first semester, and they wound up married." He shook his head. "Two kids and everything."

When he stopped, I told him a little about myself. Where I'd grown up and my first gig wrestling in New England then moving south. How I'd never been to Smoke City a week ago and wasn't sure how long I'd stay.

I thought we had a connection and wondered if other girls talked to clients like this, like talking somebody off a ledge. Was I talking myself out of a payday? Maybe other girls did have these talks, but without disclaimers about the talking not coming out of their time, so there were only a few minutes to wrestle afterward, or until the guy no longer looked at them as objects to wrestle, but still had to pay them for their time.

But I was wrong.

We hit a lull in the conversation. John sighed and took off his t-shirt. "Start on the ground?"

#

We wrestled. Half speed, less grappling than practicing the motions of a dance. I sat on his chest, facing his lower body, and he guided my hips in his hands until my butt was on his face, and he nestled in. I waited a minute and leaned forward, collapsing my thighs around his neck and squeezed softly. An erection peaked from beneath his gym shorts. He moaned Betty's name.

I figured I shouldn't correct him. We were both playing our parts. The helpless victim. The wrestler. Betty.

We transitioned through a headlock with his face in my armpit, to me scissoring his ribs between my legs while he smothered himself in my chest.

I hadn't set a timer like Madeleine had said I should on my phone. I hadn't taken out my phone at all, and it wasn't until I had him in a camel clutch, gently fish hooking his mouth, that I could see the clock radio. I'm not sure how long we'd talked or how long we'd wrestled. But I was pushing two and a half hours in the room.

"It's time," I said.

"Please."

I thought John was still playing his role, begging as he feigned extra hurt from each lightly applied hold.

No. He was begging for real. Not for mercy, but for more. "One more hold. Please."

I applied a figure-four leg lock. The thing about the hold is that it would be nearly impossible to apply in any real fight, without an opponent who was unconscious or overtly cooperating.

John was eager to cooperate.

So I lifted his leg by the ankle and threaded my leg through, spinning, positioning his ankle over the opposite knee, then my knee pit over the ankle. Apply pressure and it really does hurt. I only put on a little.

The way our bodies landed, I had my foot on his crotch and could feel him squirm.

He shuddered. He screamed his submission in a white spray of spittle. We were done.

John rested on his back while I pulled on my jeans and put my t-shirt back on, then he rolled over twice to reach a dresser drawer, pull it open and take out his wallet. He paid me in cash.

I counted the bills. Crisp twenties I imagined him taking out of the ATM for this purpose—two hundred dollars, and an extra twenty that might have been a mistake or might have been a gratuity. I didn't clarify with him, just folded them into my back pocket and got out of there.

\#

There are territories you go to to learn new skills, to build on your reputation. There are territories you go to for the money. With a little luck, you leave a little richer, your body unhurt, ready to hit the road.

I took the elevator down to the ground floor. It was odd, to go from John's panting company to the silence of the elevator to the blinking lights and chatter of the casino floor. I stopped at the first slot machine I came across, themed around woodland creatures, all squirrels and bears and birds and fauns and gnomes peeking from around tree trunks and up in leafy branches. I asked a cocktail waitress for an amaretto sour, got comfortable, and fed one of my fresh-earned twenties into the machine to take my chances.

THE GLASS CEILING

Early in the day, I met Machete Betty—Elizabeth Percy, the boss and star performer of Detroit's Motor City Mayhem Wrestling. I'd rarely worked for a woman in wrestling before, and though the territory was known for barbed wire, blood, and guts, and Betty's reputation was largely synonymous with that branding, I entered this world optimistic. Here was a chance, I thought, of a promoter who'd celebrate women's wrestling beyond its capacity for T&A, and who probably wouldn't try to sleep with me.

I was caught off guard by how small she was. I knew she wasn't a giant, but I'd pictured her at three inches taller than me, not three inches shorter. She was thinner than I'd imagined, too. Narrower at the shoulders. She was already in her wrestling gear. Management who worked double duty, wrestling themselves, had a habit of dressing early, knowing there may not be time later. Her arms and legs were all muscle and sinew but more tightly packed. Her abdomen was concave and rippled with small stomach muscles. She was unmistakably cut but also had a fragile quality to her.

"New girl," she addressed me, though days before we'd spoken on the phone and she'd acknowledged me by name, talked up her favorite matches of mine with Lacey

Lipsmack and Susy Hamilton. I'd been anything but anonymous to her then. Not a *new girl*, but a star she was lucky to sign. But in that moment, in her makeshift office, partitioned from the rest of the locker room with collapsible cubicle walls, Machete Betty fingered a razor blade and told me, "I wish I could slice open your head and let all your ideas spill out here on my desk."

Her desk was a card table adorned with a big, boxy laptop, a knee brace, a red Sharpie on top of 8x10s she'd sign for the fans who lined up to meet her before the show. She had her combat boots on, propped up on the table, one ankle crossed over the other.

"But since I can't, I guess I'll settle for slicing you," she said. "It's you and me in the semi-main tonight."

Betty was known for soliciting ideas from her talents— bleeding them dry Lou Lapinski had warned me when he heard I was heading for Motor City. I said I was thankful I'd get to have some input. A lot of bookers were control freaks, least likely of all to listen to a woman's ideas.

Lou said to be careful.

Motor City Mayhem was also known for barbed wire, baseball bats, thumbtacks, firecrackers. The territory had gone viral for a clip of Machete Betty gouging a guy's forehead with a ninja star until it sprayed blood. All this blood and guts stuff had come into vogue in the States in the 1990s, become passe after the novelty wore off, then come back around, not so much in the mainstream wrestling on cable TV, but for niche audiences who lovingly chanted *you sick fuck! you sick fuck!* after particularly sadistic displays.

I told Betty I was looking forward to it, and whether she took it at face value or saw through the bravado, that night, I found the same razor blade she'd fingered in conversation pressed just beneath my hairline at ringside. The stab was one thing. It was the drag of the blade, not so much slicing as tearing a jagged line through my skin that hurt. I cried out, kicking my legs. No telling if Betty knew I was hurt and kept going or thought I was selling. No telling if she cared.

Two men in the front row cheered. One gray haired, round around the middle. The other much younger, with broad shoulders, a cobra tattoo coiled around his upper arm. They both wore white t-shirts, in incongruent tie-dyed red patterns.

Not tie-dyed. I'd heard of this. A custom among Moter City Mayhem's most devout apostles. Shirts stained with blood from shows. Living art. The fans' greatest hope they'd get to add to the design at the next gorey show.

Betty pulled me along by the hair, not the kind of gentle tug where she led the way and seta a pace the way veterans wrestlers typically knew to. Typically, veterans weren't out to hurt anyone.

I not so much crawled as scuttled, dripping blood. Betty yanked upward, so I knelt as high as I could, high enough so my head rose above the ringside railing. High enough to rub my forehead into the old man's stomach, while he let out a guttural *yeah!*

#

I didn't expect a lot of facetime with the boss. Some bookers make a show out of taking a new talent out to lunch. But that's all lip service. The illusion of what the relationship will be like, because a young wrestler might put stock in such things and they've really connected with the boss. It can buy weeks, even months of goodwill before they realize that ending every night counting the arena lights isn't an anomaly but their station in the promotion, just another body for someone more important to mow through.

The fact Machete Betty worked with me my first night in Detroit meant something to me. More than Cobb salads and iced teas. Call me naïve but it felt like there was substance to us spilling blood together (she'd let me hardway her with the edge of the ring bell—a hope spot by the standards of Motor City Mayhem, signaling to fans maybe I'd get one over on her before she finished me off).

After I got my stitches—Motor City Mayhem was ahead of the curve of a lot of the indies in having a medic on hand at every show, though the style of wrestling also made it necessary—Betty invited me back to her place.

I opened the camera on my phone and switched to selfie mode to study the stitches, to get a sense of how I looked—an absurdity before entering a party of wrestlers, let alone ones from Motor City Mayhem.

The dashed line had already settled from a bright red to shade closer to maroon. I looked like Frankenstein's monster.

Half the roster was there. Dory Prichard and Terry Brisco flanked Betty. They worked a tag team gimmick as The Plaintiffs, constantly trying to sue their opponents for wrongdoing, only to earn more righteous ass-kickings the next time around. Abraham Woods, the men's heavyweight champion's gargantuan frame overflowed from an easy chair. His girlfriend Crystal curled up on him. They alternated sips off the same beer, and when they finished the first, she fetched another, not having to ask where they were in the fridge or where to find the bottle opener. Not asking permission.

Wolly Ringmold, with her hair dyed clown red held court over a game of Texas Hold 'Em seated next to Misty Jay whom I hardly recognized, stripped of her red white and blue face paint, her star-spangled sports bra, hiding her body away behind an oversized Rammstein t-shirt. To her other side, a three-hundred-pound bruiser with long scars all over his forehead, next to him Demetrius Tyler who I'd shared a locker room with down south years back. If he remembered me, he didn't show any signs of it. A little-person wrestler who went by Cannonball, known for wrapping himself in barbed wire and charging larger opponents' stomachs, and a beefy Hawaiian who wrestled as Slamma Jamma filled out the table.

Someone prepared a ice cube tray full of cherry Jello shots, but only Betty ate from it, which led me to wonder if it were her exclusive property and everyone knew not to dig their grubby fingers into it, or if it's simply that she was the only one who liked cherry Jello shots, but someone knew to have them ready for the boss. She dug in, like she was excavating shallow graves each time and licked the sticky sweet red dots from her fingertips after.

Same end table, beside the jello shots, a glass ramekin. Inside, Betty's razor, soaking in the stench of rubbing alcohol to cleanse the blade of my blood.

"The future's all digital," Betty said. "We don't need TV, pay-per-view. Anyone chasing the old models is a dinosaur now."

I'd heard this narrative before. A lot of indie promoters without the resources to broadcast by traditional means had labeled the Internet the great equalizer, the opportunity to get hooked on their product. Indeed, I, like most people—workers and marks alike— had first encountered Motor City Mayhem on YouTube.

"You have to have a strategy, though," Betty went on. "People don't understand. They think someone watches a video online and that's going to get them to—what—order a DVD? They don't understand that digital is *it*. And it's not going to make anyone the next WWE. But if you carve your own niche, that's where the power lies."

Betty's model was deceptively complicated. She recorded everything but released selectively in curated episodes of varying length to tell the stories she meant to. Workers didn't know half the time if they were working the continuation of an existing storyline or reshooting the same match over. The most devout fans knew. They didn't wait for Motor City Mayhem to make its two-to-three week loop back to their nearest bingo hall. They followed the traveling circus in its two-to-three hour radius to see it all live, to capture their own footage on smart phones.

"That's part of the fun. The die-hards watch all the fan footage and speculate about what's going to become canon. You have to give them something to wonder about. Something to have an opinion about."

"And then you give them what they want," I said.

Betty smiled. "I know what's best for the fans."

\#

Same match. Same razor.

The next time I wrestled Machete Betty, we worked a lot of the same spots, though this time she sliced my upper arm instead of my head, giving it time to heal. Accordingly, once there was blood, she focused her attack, working a Fujiwara armbar, a keylock, variations on kimuras that weren't entirely logical in sequence of what part of the arm she punished at any given moment, but all drew attention to the source from which my blood was flowing.

We worked a different kind of hope spot this time, when I got her in a triangle choke, squeezing her neck and left arm between my thighs. I'd busted her lip open prior and the way she writhed and made it look like she had internal bleeding.

A girl—seven, maybe eight years old—stood by her father at ringside. She wore a purple John Cena t-shirt, and I understood this to be a family outing. How different could independent wrestling be from what they saw on TV? Fewer stars, maybe, but the same family friendly high spots off the top ropes, heels begging off, babyfaces flexing their muscles and slapping high fives with the fans at ringside. Ringside seats available for twenty bucks. What a deal!

The girl stood. The man sat. They were about the same height that way, his hand on her shoulder, trying to decide if they should go. Was it all too violent? Would she be sad she didn't get to stay for the main event?

I gave the girl a wink. Meant as a reassurance it'd all be OK. Kayfabe be damned. No reason to be afraid.

The girl propped her feet on the lower edge of the railing to stand two inches taller and leaned over the railing, as close the ring as she could get. She opened her mouth. She screamed.

"Powerbomb that bitch!"

A man, not her father, agreed. "Yeah, powerbomb that bitch."

The words gathered steam. Spreading. There couldn't be more than a three, maybe four hundred people but some amalgamation of their enthusiasm and the acoustics of the little arena make the sound deafening as the crowd chanted, *Powerbomb that bitch! Powerbomb that bitch!*

In the ring, Betty caught my eye. She didn't have to whisper to hide it when she spoke to me—the crowd was that loud. "You heard the people."

She was up. The powerbomb—hefting me up and throwing me down—was a legitimate counter to escape a triangle choke, though in a real fight, there was a danger of the choke sinking in deeper. But this was pro wrestling.

Betty powerbombed me, her form collapsing on top of mine as we both sold exhaustion. She did knock the wind out of me and I had to still myself, to gasp air back into my lungs.

The chant was still going

Betty got back to her feet, head still between my legs. Hands locked with mine. I'd done this spot before—the consecutive powerbombs, and it was about sixty percent her strength in getting me back up, the other forty percent my core and my control in getting myself back up so I was seated on her shoulders, so she could powerbomb me again.

I landed a little higher on my neck and the back of my head.

The chant ended.

A new one took its place. A normal chant for a wrestling show. So commonplace that it felt out of place in Motor City Mayhem.

One more time! One more time!

Betty's hair hung over her face when she bent in close. "You good?"

I squeezed her hand.

I rose again.

One more time!

I fell.

I lolled my head to the side, to the girl in the John Cena t-shirt. Her fists uppercutted through the air. An expression of delight.

\#

A lot of the Motor City Mayhem crew went out to the bar. A dive bar. A good bar, because the roster was all regulars and fans who went there were content to exist in the same bar space without feeling the need to beg for autographs or selfies or make awkward conversation about all the inner workings of a match.

We were left to our own devices, and Betty and I wound up alone in a booth. She was the boss, so she got the side of the booth covered in cracked navy blue vinyl. I took the side that was all exposed wood.

Betty swirled a tumbler of whiskey in one hand, fingered her razor in the other. "It's funny, I tried to kill myself with this razor once." Before I had the chance to react—to ask questions, to express condolences, she let go of the whiskey and turned her wrist upward to show me the shock of white lines. "I use it in wrestling because wrestling saved me."

She pushed on, no beat in between, no further segue, to ask me, "How did you wind up wrestling?"

I told her the Cliff Notes version I'd cultivated between small talk with other wrestlers, with the fans. The story a daydream version of myself tells to talk show hosts when I'm driving into the night, well past the point everyone back home would be asleep. I tell her about watching Stone Cold Steve Austin take a choke slam from Kane, then getting up to keep on fighting. I tell her about the boyfriend I staged a steel cage match with at a tennis court. He'd outgrown wrestling. I guess I'd outgrown him because I wasn't sad about leaving him behind to train and work my first territory. I was electrified by the possibilities.

"That's it," Betty cut in. "The possibilities. You know the critics say Motor City Mayhem is just chaos—just the bunch of guys hitting each other, cutting each other, burning each other with whatever we can find. They say, *oh, there just happened to be a glass panel* lying around, how convenient someone took a spinebuster straight through it. But that shit's not contrived. That's what happens when the only limits to what happens in the ring are your imagination. Screw the bullshit rulebook. Screw convention."

Across the bar, Abraham threw a dart, but not the straight ahead point out, sailing way a dart ordinarily flies. He threw it like a knife, clumsily flipping end over end. It hit the dartboard lengthwise, bounced off the cork and clattered to the floor. So he tried again. The third time, it stuck, albeit to the black cork surrounding the board. No points earned. But he'd done it his own way. Wolly was up after him. She threw her dart the same way.

"Do you know how I got started?" Betty asked. "I'm third-generation, you know."

I didn't know. It occurred to me I'd never considered how Machete Betty got her start in wrestling. She was a major name on the indies—a performer I'd heard of when I broke in, and a name that got passed around as a promoter after I was in the business, journeymen talking about what a nutjob she could be, or praising the creative latitude she gave her performers. I worked with a guy in

St. Louis for a while who said he'd slept with her, but he said he'd slept with a lot of people.

"My daddy was Arnie Falk. You know him, right? Midcard talent, then he started promoting shows around Seattle. Learned it from his father, Bubba Parry."

I knew the Bubba Parry to Arnie Falk line. There was a third-generation tag team in that family tree who'd had a brief run with WWE. Everybody knows the families of wrestling—not like the old days when they'd often as not obscure those connections. In the age of the Internet there are no secrets. In an age of sequels and remakes every legacy lets their story be known, not a new star, the continuation of a story.

But I'd never heard about Betty's tie to them.

"Maybe I should say, I was Arnie Falk's bastard daughter. A mishap. Mama tried to let him know he was pregnant, worked every connection she could find, but never got a hold of him until he was traveling back through the Midwest. She had me by then. A little girl in the flesh. And here Arnie'd already missed the first few months of my life."

I sipped from my beer. A stout I hadn't really wanted, but I'd misunderstood what beer I was getting when I ordered from the list on the chalkboard, or else the bartender misheard me. It was thick, dark, opaque. "I was always sort of jealous of people who got to grow up around the business. My family never got—"

"He didn't stick around," Betty said. "And he skipped out on the next Midwest loop. Mom brought me to the matches to try to see him, but when she finally got to talk to some of the boys, they said he was home injured. One of them said he'd hurt his ankle. Another one said it was neck."

I knew the rest of this story. Hang around wrestling long enough and you hear variations on it. Not everyone's daddy was a wrestler, but you don't have to be a wrestler to hurt someone. To leave them behind. To make you want to leave them behind.

Betty was the forgotten daughter. Her mother didn't press things after the first year or two. She didn't lie to Betty about who her father was, though. The truth was, her mom was still a wrestling fan despite everything, so Betty grew up one too and before she understood everything that had happened between her mother and father, she already knew she wanted to be a wrestler. I asked if she'd ever confronted her Arnie. Wrestling's a small world after all. Hang around it long enough and everyone crosses paths with everyone else.

Betty said she hadn't. Because why would she? Eighteen years of her life, he'd known where to find her if he wanted to. And if he wanted her now? Now that she was a wrestler. A promoter. A damn good one. What right did he have to call himself her father now?

She got a faraway look. Looking past me. Looking halfway across the country at her daddy. Looking back through time. "I became a wrestler because *fuck you*, that's why," she said. "I did it because I could. Because everybody wants to talk about the glass ceilings life throws over your head, so you can see where you want to go, but you can never quite get there. Fuck that. I've never been scared of a little broken glass."

\#

Our next match was about glass.

See the glass panel. Accept it. No more contrived than baseball bats, leather straps, a wrestling ring itself when all someone needs for a fight is an empty space. It's all contrivance and it's not in any given object's presence, but in the attempts to rationalize it that absurdity lies.

The glass panel appeared. The glass panel got propped, one side on the ring apron, one side on the barricade. The barricade was positioned five and a half feet from ringside—a good foot further out than usual in Motor City Mayhem, leaving more exposed cement floor around the padding at ringside.

We started the story not so different from our matches leading up to this point. Betty cocky, playing to the crowd on her entrance. She didn't see it coming when I snuck up from behind, ring bell in hand, and knock her the fuck out. She sold like she was unconscious while I pulled the glass panel from beneath the ring. The referee acted like he was trying to stop me, trying to take this thing away from me while really he shouldered half the weight, steadied the unwieldy object, helped get it in position before I pie faced him out of the way. I turned to the crowd on the ring apron, beside the panel. *I'm going to piledrive this bitch straight through!*

Betty was resourceful, though. Only the diehards, the extra observant fans, or those lucky to, out of happenstance, cast an eye aside while I was drawing their attention would notice when Betty rolled out to ringside on the far side then slid underneath the ring altogether.

The devout audience knew the piledriver wasn't happening. Not yet at least. The big props never get put to immediate use, spoiling all the tension around them. We'll fake it first. Make the fans wait and forget it's there.

It's Chekhov's gun. It'll come back around.

In the meantime, I sold confusion at the empty ring. *Betty's disappeared!*

Betty reappeared. She wielded a fluorescent light tube in each hand.

The moments to follow were a flurry. Betty swung the tubes expertly, less like baseball bats than nunchucks, whirling, looking as though they bent in motion. I begged off, ducked, and dodged until she had me backed into a corner. The audience fell silent, because no noise could aptly communicate their excitement. In mainstream wrestling, the aggressor might be duped—lulled into distraction, only for the would-be victim to escape or reverse the momentum of the action, gain control, casting the most vicious weapons aside.

In Motor City Mayhem, it was the carnage and viscera that were inevitable. The first tube exploded against my thigh, and the blood trickled from it immediately. The next shattered against my shoulder.

I did regain the advantage, though, against the wishes of a crowd that was all in on Machete Betty. When she ducked her head, I did *piledrive this bitch* to the mat, then again on the floor at ringside. She rolled, helpless. She took shelter beneath the glass panel.

I stood on the panel, looking down at Betty's gasping form. This was the part of our plan I was least confident in—that the glass floor wouldn't give out beneath my weight.

I thought I heard a crack. No matter. It only had to hold a second longer. Maybe it helped that the glass had started to give way when Betty rose up, straight through it to get a hold of me. Glass everywhere. Her face painted scarlet. I only rose as high as my knees before she hooked each of my arms, my head to her side and drilled me headfirst into the shards below.

The rest was all epilogue, the story told, the show at an end. Betty gathered me up and rolled me beneath the bottom rope, back into the ring. I played dead as she army crawled on top of me for the pin. She exhaled. I inhaled. A sliver of glass wedged itself into the palm of the referee's hand when he the mat. He hesitated a beat but carried on to hit the canvas twice more.

Betty helped me to my feet after the match—a rare show of collegiality in front of the fans, but our story together was done we embraced and left the ring arm in arm before taking a victory lap around ringside rubbing our faces on every white t-shirt we could find until we'd stanched the bleeding.

WHEN SANTA CLAUS
CAME TO TOWN

It was fall—a ruddy point in mid-October when the romantic crisp crackle of fallen leaves turned to muddy debris and it was impossible to set foot outside without making a mess of your shoes. Mid-October, when the rains started, and though there was no promise of snow, there was nonetheless a chill in the air in the Pacific Northwest when Santa Claus came to town.

He had an old school look, more of the Dusty Rhodes pudge than the John Cena bodybuilder physique that was in vogue by the mid-2000s. But he could go—strong, agile, quick in ways that allowed him to execute his "Sleigh Bell" running power slam with great efficacy.

And as much as some of the crew backstage balked at the outdated trope of a wrestling Santa—the kind of character only a kid could buy into and who undermined the sportier and edgier directions wrestling had taken from the mid-1990s on, Santa made friends easily in the locker room, passing around extra candy canes from the stash he'd distribute to kids at ringside before his match and then a flask of whiskey. He got us all good and knackered by the end of the night, even Simon Schwartz, the Jewish booker who so rarely partook in extracurriculars with the talent.

It was probably the booze that emboldened Robbie Sundance, the young cowboy outlaw heel, to finger the ends of Santa's big, white beard and comment that it looked so real.

Quick as a flicker of light on silver tinsel, Santa spun Robbie around, locked a bicep over his throat in a chokehold and told him never to touch his beard again.

Santa let him go with a *ho ho ho* and everybody laughed, all that tension evaporating into something like Christmas cheer. Even Robbie, red-faced as he was, got in a chuckle and joined in singing along to "Rudolph the Red-Nosed Reindeer."

#

There was a Christmas I spent blind in one eye. I'd already been playing hurt to sell a particularly brutal beatdown from my arch-rival Becky Olbeck. I'd come to the ring on crutches with a cast around my arm, selling an injury that, were it real, wouldn't have allowed me to support myself on crutches. In particularly villainous fashion, Becky took one of the crutches from me. The never say die heroine, I hopped on one foot and tried to fend her off with the other crutch until she slammed hers against the side of my head and I crumpled to the mat.

Spots like that are tricky, because you've got to execute quickly for them not to look phony as hell. But they're dangerous, too. Becky didn't hit my eye, but she hit my head hard and though I hugged her and said it was fine backstage, I nonetheless woke in my bed later that night with a big black spot in my line of vision.

The doctors said it was blood. More than likely a busted vessel from the impact of getting hit. Nothing to do but rest and wait it out.

I was already unhappy with my role in the promotion—even if I hadn't been hurt, I was positioned as a stepping stone for Becky to get to a title shot. Besides that, there was the matter of being away from home for Christmas. Not my first time, but before I'd been working, celebrating the holiday in a locker room. This Christmas, I didn't have the money to travel, besides which I didn't fancy having to defend myself from behind an eye patch when Mom started one of her tirades about how wrestling was no way for a woman to make a living.

And then there was the matter of Ricky Youngblood, the broad-shouldered Hawaiian with a six pack and a penchant for writing Shakespearean sonnets. It seemed like a dream that I'd landed him for a boyfriend, and I was experienced enough in the business, let alone in life, not to expect for it to last forever. Still, I hadn't been prepared for how abruptly it would end. I lost him to blond-haired, blue-eyed Alice Andrews, watching him fall in love with her with each hold he showed her backstage and each time I caught one of them rubbing the other's sore shoulders. I could have gone old school, slapped her in a hammerlock, slammed her against a locker, told her to keep her hands off my man, but I'd always told myself I wouldn't be that sort of schoolyard bully that wrestling locker rooms perpetuated, besides which I could see that those same soft features that allowed her to sell and get such sympathy in the ring would make her the victim backstage, and any bruise I gave her would only drive her trembling deeper into Ricky's arms.

Missing shows, missing nights at the bar afterward, I didn't have any illusions that Ricky wasn't necking with her in the back of a car or sleeping with her at a motel where he and I'd shared a room months earlier.

I spent Christmas alone in my studio apartment, cable versions of Christmas movies on the tube television until watching out of one eye was too irritating to bear, then unplugging the tree because its twinkling lights felt mocking. I threw away the chocolates Ricky bought me before he left for the big Christmas show, because the fact that Christmas once had been my favorite holiday made everything about that Christmas more miserable. I closed my eye, lay on the couch, and waited for it all to be over.

#

Santa went on an undefeated streak. In those early outings, he was billed under variations like Father Christmas and Chris Kringle and Old Saint Nick. But in the end, he was simply Santa Claus.

Santa was undefeated up to that point—harmless holiday fun, beating up on the lower card guys and fresh faces who didn't stand to lose much dropping a fall to a novelty act in matches no one would remember. But Simon had bigger plans of Santa beating progressively bigger names those weeks to come in an undefeated streak that would build to Christmas Eve.

"Santa Claus challenges for the title, Christmas Eve." Simon stretched his arms up over his head and waved them slowly as if he could make the marquee materialize through sheer force of will. "And here's the biggest twist of all: Santa wins."

It was unheard of for someone who'd just come into the territory to win the top prize so quickly. Of course, Simon would explain, that was the idea.

Maybe it's because Santa shared his liquor so liberally, or because it was hard to be threatened by someone working a gimmick unlike any other in the locker room, but no one objected to the plan. Even Race Davidson, the reigning champ, nodded along, especially after Simon laid out how he'd win the title back at the next show, Santa weakened by the absence of Christmas magic, and set to go off on his way—maybe to return a year later if the holiday angle did big business this time around.

Santa didn't seem so sure. "Won't kids get confused about me wrestling on Christmas Eve? When I'm supposed to deliver presents?"

Simon laughed him off, but for the first time I could recall, Santa didn't seem so jolly. I could understand trepidations about lesser championships—after you've won one and feel validated in your profession, you balk at having to carry the extra weight of the belt around in your luggage from town to town. The top title's different, though, if only for the main event paycheck that comes with it.

Santa snapped out of his funk soon enough, though, and passed around his flask again as Simon explained his more immediate plans for who'd wrestle whom in the weeks ahead.

#

There was another Christmas, not so sad. I was the reigning women's champion in a territory that operated on the San Diego-Mexico border that made no bones about fudging work vs. tourist visas and having people get across that border by any means necessary to serve fans on both sides of it. In a land where lucha libre was king, I'd been well received for working a hybrid style, because I could grapple but also fly off the top rope.

Because I could muscle up smaller luchadoras and also keep up with them in sprints.

I felt vindicated that Christmas.

And I was dating the Campeon Del Universo, Manuel Santana.

It was a top regional title, built up to sound like a world title for an audience that didn't much care that it wasn't. We worked shows in small venues, but in front of some of the most passionate fans I'd seen. *True believers* I was told, and though I don't know that they all succumbed to the stereotypes of fans who don't realize wrestling is fixed, I do know that grandmothers banged their canes against the barricade front row, every bit as committed to the story in the ring as the grandchildren in foil masks at their sides.

Most of us worked short matches that Christmas show. No one was expected to go all out. We played the greatest hits and were on our way, my match a five-minute, four-way sprint that I hardly broke a sweat over.

But Manuel insisted on going long. He insisted on blading—cutting his forehead deep to give the fans a bloody show—in his battle with Barbaro. The muscle-bound heel wrestled in furry tights and didn't have much in his offensive repertoire past clubbing forearm blows and a bear hug.

Manuel made him look like a million bucks.

Backstage, I told Manuel he didn't need to work so hard on Christmas.

He asked what better gift he could give to the people?

Afterward, we went out on the beach. Never mind the relative cold. There was colder beer and someone grilled burgers and we all had a good time. Fans found us there, or maybe followed us. I'd learned long before that, unlike other territories, these wrestlers didn't see the die-hard fans as nuisances at the border, nor as marks to take advantage of by having them buy us drinks or pay for photos. They were family. That's what Manuel always said, never declining an autograph request, gleefully throwing a glow in the dark Frisbee with kids as if he, too were a child.

We sang "Jingle Bells" and "Frosty the Snowman" and at one point the wind kicked up, sending sand into swirling squalls. Squint your eyes and you might convince yourself it was a blizzard.

And all at once I missed home. In that sentimental, nonsensical way, because I knew if I were home I'd only fight with my mother and grow tired of my father's insistence on lecturing me against a backdrop of rock 'n' roll records we'd listened to together since I was a pre-teen. I knew the coffee would be weak because they always used the grounds twice and the house would be dim for all the bulbs they didn't bother to change.

And yet it was home.

I may have been happier by most any measure on that beach. But I was three thousand miles from home.

#

Santa's beard and hair were real. He'd turned his curse into a blessing, because going white-haired in his thirties had at least allowed him to play Santa in the ring and rake in a few extra bucks working shopping mall photo ops when times were lean.

The two of us wound up sitting side by side on a locker room bench one night, after I'd wrestled but before I'd hit the showers, before he'd gone to the ring for his semi-main event bout. He asked me about how long I'd been wrestling and where I'd come from, punctuated with a compliment that I was one of the best lady workers he'd seen. I'm not sure why it had taken me so long to ask his own story. He was vaguer in his responses, telling me he was from here and there, before rattling off territories where he'd worked that ranged from the Mid-South to the Great Plains to New England, to residencies in Mexico, Japan, and Germany. Then he told me he'd always meant to find his way back here to the Pacific Northwest.

I asked what was so great about it? The gray skies? The rain? The budding hipster population?

He laughed a *ho ho ho* and said he'd known a girl here when he was much younger. If you wanted to wrestle at the highest levels, you couldn't be picky about where you plied your trade. "But," he said, "it's good to be home for the holidays."

#

Was it a single conversation that put me in Santa's car? There's little tracking how road marriages come together in wrestling, but we got on well enough that he invited me into his big red Buick to head to the next town and we went on from there. He had a collection of scratched up CDs wedged in the space between the radio and the temperature controls. Maybe it was the season or the gimmick, but he didn't seem to have anything but Christmas music, and so Christmas music we listened to.

I got to know him the way that only so many hours in a confined space facilitates. It wasn't until our third long drive together, late night, headed north over ice-slicked roads that he told me about his boy Julie.

"Of course he doesn't go by Julie anymore," Santa said over a skipping track of Mel Torme singing "Have Yourself a Merry Little Christmas." Santa paused at the line when Mel sang, *through the years, we all will be together*, no telling if it were happenstance or he knew the song well enough to time it just so. "It's Julius now. Or I think I heard his mother call him Jules once, when he was bugging her when I had her on the phone."

Santa didn't have to tell me Julius was the real reason he'd considered the Pacific Northwest home, but did catch me off guard when he explained that, if things went right—if he could stay in the mother's good graces, this would be the first Christmas Eve he'd get to spend with him that the boy would remember, out of infancy, a full-on child now who might wonder at Santa Claus sitting at the dinner table with his family or playing with him after, or—again, if everything went right with Julius's mother—reveal himself to be the kid's father.

I reminded Santa about his Christmas Eve title shot.

Santa took a long, slurping sip from his gas station coffee. He'd pumped in an obscene amount of peppermint creamer—sweet enough to make my teeth hurt thinking about it. He skipped to the next song—a punk version of "Rudolph The Red-Nosed Reindeer"—and didn't say another word.

#

Had it not been for that last conversation about Christmas Eve, I may have been even more surprised when Santa dropped me off at the back entrance of the arena rather than parking the car to come inside himself.

"You've got to come in," I said. "You're the main event. You're getting the title."

He gripped the wheel and stared straight ahead. I thought he might take off with me still in the car, less malice or impatience than sheer distraction. That he'd given me the ride and was dropping me off at all were kindnesses.

"I can make it," he said. "An hour drive there, two—two and a half hours tops at the house before Julie's bedtime, then forty-five minutes back if I drive fast and get a break on lights. I'm back for the main event easy."

He'd thought it through. "Tell them I'm on my way," he said. Then, more sure, back in the full Santa persona, "Old Saint Nick always delivers on Christmas Eve," and, as I shut the passenger side door behind me, a hearty, "Ho! Ho! Ho!"

\#

Simon wasn't so sure of Santa's reliability, Christmas Eve or not. He panicked when Santa wasn't there by the time the audience started filing in.

There are certain unspoken rules about what stays between the wrestlers on the road, and what we'll tell a promoter. But under the circumstances, I told Simon what I knew.

Simon came after me first—for letting Santa drive off like that and then for not saying something sooner. The heat was off me soon enough, though, as Simon called Santa's phone and left a voicemail with demands to *call me back*, and the caveat that *the only excuse not to pick up when I call is that you've got a death grip on the wheel, going a-hundred-ten to get to the goddamn arena, fuck-knuckle*. He delegated responsibilities to the boys to keep calling and to text while he called over the champ to mull over backup plans for who could challenge for the title (New York Nick Nettles? Too obvious. Dan Sally? Too vanilla.), not to mention the question of whether the title would still change hands.

I left for my match. The arena was toasty as if to overcompensate for the blustery night. Cindy Grinds and I both broke a sweat on the initial lockup, and as much as we tried to sell our perspiration as a sign of hard-fought battle, the crowd didn't care. One of the dangers of a show built so purely around its main event was that no one gave more than half-hearted attention to any match except for Santa's title fight.

By the time I made it backstage, though, there was a new plan. Santa was out. They'd tell the tale that champion Race Davidson had commissioned the Grinch to sabotage Santa's sleigh, so not only would he not be able to make it to the arena, but Christmas itself was as good as cancelled. The cocky champ would laugh out loud then go so far as to offer an open challenge to anyone who wanted to try to take the title off him. Scrappy underdog Luke Walsh, from nowhere near the title picture, already tired from losing earlier in the night, would answer the call and in a Christmas miracle, catch a crossbody block off the top rope to steal the pin and go home with the belt.

Of course, I didn't hear the game plan in such straightforward fashion, just the debate about whether Walsh were believable at all and where things would go from there and, even if he lost the title right back, if him winning it at all that would tarnish the belt's credibility? (*Tarnish it more than Santy Claus winning?* another voice chimed in.)

I wasn't at the arena when Walsh won the title.

Before the match got underway, I drove to the jail.

One of the boys gets arrested, they might've called the booker in a move equal parts designed to explain himself, and because the booker may well be the only one who has bail money to spare. For all of Santa's errors in judgment that night, he had the presence of mind to know that Simon would've let him rot in his cell.

I had just enough money to spot him. It was foolish to spend all my cash, but it was Christmas Eve and I was the one Santa Claus had turned to.

After I got him, Santa and I pulled over at a gas station with a sitting area. He bought me a chocolate-frosted doughnut and told me the tale.

It'd been his greatest wish to spend Christmas Eve with Julius, but he hadn't spent those weeks in the territory leading up to that night getting closer to his family, making inroads. Rather, he'd watched from a distance and scouted out the house. He didn't call first, but rather parked down the street, took a hearty swig from his flask, then marched to their door. Julius's mother smelled the alcohol on him and told him to get lost. The rest was a blur of yelling and having the door shut in his face and kicking it down and stealing a fleeting look at his son. Santa wasn't certain if his ex-wife had called the police on him or if it had been a neighbor, only that no one had much interest in his side of the story.

Santa raised his coffee cup to me, something like saying cheers. "Merry Christmas, right?"

It was too dark outside, too bright under the fluorescent lights in the seating area of the gas station to see past the glass into the night. Rather, we were stuck with a reflection of ourselves. I hadn't had a chance to shower between wrestling and getting his call, and had thrown on the t-shirt and jeans I'd worn to the arena and borrowed somebody's car. I'd have to bring the car back and wasn't sure if I'd have to answer for where I'd gone or on Santa's behalf. Watching the two of us, I suspected he wouldn't return to the arena. He may not return to working the territory at all, depending on how far the night's arrest would let him go. Better to shave the beard, dye his hair, move on to a promoter who'd never guess he'd played Santa Claus before.

"Everyone's got a past they're running from," I thought out loud.

Santa shook his head. "Some folks are running toward the future."

#

I had a Christmas future. A husband I hadn't met yet. We had a kid together, too, who kept me off the road for a while. I wasn't sure how I felt about that.

It's Christmas now and our boy, Miles is three, which it turns out makes him just mobile enough to be dangerous all the time. Sturdy enough to walk, tall enough to reach up into the Christmas tree and find an ornament shaped like Santa Claus.

I watch him in the haze of a house too warm from the gas heating, windows frosted, strings of light shining bright not only across the branches, but in swooping, uneven parabolas from the ceiling.

Quick as a snap suplex, Miles catches Santa and pulls him free and it's hard to tell if it's my cry for him to stop that startles him, or if he'd have dropped the thing anyway. The only thing for certain is that the ornament breaks on the floor, fracturing into five discrete pieces and an indeterminate amount of dust.

No sharp edges, though. No great expense. Just a bargain-bin Santa. A disposable thing.

Miles turns red and holds his breath a second, the preamble to crying, but I hold him close.

"Don't worry about it, baby."

My back has a chronic wrestler's ache. I'm as tired as any mother left to fend for herself for long stretches, my husband still making towns, still taking slams. Miles sniffles and rubs his nose on the shoulder of my sweater the way a boy his age doesn't know any better than to do. I tell him not to worry about a thing.

ONWARD

I recognized Dylan by his eyes, scanning the diner from the entryway, by the hostess station where I watched a skinny little woman in the teal and white dress ask how many were in his party. He was the same height when I'd seen him last, but, if anything, he looked a little skinnier, except around the middle where a middle-aged paunch had set in. His hair had thinned.

I waved to him. He waved back, recognizing me on sight. I didn't have to look the same to him. He'd seen YouTube clips of me—the impetus for reconnecting when he looked me up under my real name and messaged me over Facebook. We'd traded messages on and off for a year. I'd thought of connecting the next time I passed through his area but thought better of it. No one wants to ask her high school boyfriend if he wants to meet up and get rejected. But he messaged me afterward to ask why I hadn't messaged him, after footage surfaced from a match I'd had in Syracuse. It told him it'd slipped my mind, but I'd catch him the next time through.

We hugged. "You look great," he said, and I was thankful the black eye I'd sported two weeks earlier had faded, that I hadn't needed any stitches since. The fluorescent lights in an all-night diner like this tended to expose things, and I looked all right on this loop back toward my hometown.

I lied and told him he looked great too, gripping his hands after we'd let go of the hug. We sat down on opposite sides of the booth, laminated menus between us, a little iron holster for catsup, maple syrup, sugar, Sweet'N Low, salt, and pepper.

"You've got kids." I blurted it out. His wife and kids were the signature differences from when I'd left after graduation to wrestle. This diner was a good forty-minute drive from Shermantown, where we'd grown up, where he'd stayed. The closest I wanted to come to Shermantown, because I'd discovered when trips home were sporadic, everyone wants a piece of you and there are hurt feelings for anyone you didn't make time for.

Dylan pulled out his phone and scrolled through photos. There was something boyish about how excited he was to show off his kids. I'd already seen the first one he showed me. "That's Malcolm, our little dare devil." In this one, they were in a proper photo studio. Malcolm was maybe a year old? I didn't have the best sense of age around kids that little. He belied the collared shirt-sweater-vest-khakis-loafers his parents had dressed him up in, crawling on the floor toward the camera, head cocked up with a smile that could only be described as mischievous. Dylan was fuzzy, leaning forward from a stool, reaching. Wendy, his wife was a little clearer. She sat back, head back, open-mouthed laughing in a way that seemed posed to me, but maybe the photographer caught her in just the right moment.

We went to high school with Wendy. I didn't really know her. She was two years younger than us.

Two years would've felt like a big deal then—a senior dating a sophomore, or a guy in community college dating a high school senior. Put it in the context of a marriage with school-aged kids. Put it in the context of a life and two years was nothing at all. Case in point, when I got charged with wrestling a girl, five, six years younger, older, it didn't matter at all. She was a worker of my generation who got in the business around the same time, watched the same wrestlers growing up, had likely as not traveled through the same territories, working under the same promoters, just in a different sequence. We knew the same people. Two years was no difference at all.

Kids were a difference. Doesn't matter how old. A change in identity. I'd known the Dylan whose dad watched wrestling, so he watched wrestling. Now, he was Dylan, first and foremost, dad to these kids who watched wrestling too. Dylan showed me the photos to corroborate, no telling if the focus on wrestling was for my benefit, or organic because his kids were as wrestle-crazed as the two of us once were.

"The funny thing is, I'd stopped watching. I mean, you and me finish high school and we're at the pinnacle—The Rock, Stone Cold. Then, what? John Cena. I'd still check out WrestleMania if I remembered it was happening or if someone was having a party, but that was it."

I remembered a party. Curt Wojtanowski—a fair-weather fan if there ever was one—hosted a get together for WrestleMania 17, the one where Stone Cold Steve Austin beat The Rock but had to turn heel to do it, beating his opponent over and over with a steel chair. Curt gave me a hard time because, unlike the other girls, I wasn't there just because my boyfriend liked wrestling. I liked wrestling, and he lorded it over me that girls don't really like wrestling, like he knew more about it than me because he'd watched in his tighty-whities when Hulk Hogan beat The Macho Man and now he was watching again when wrestling was back in style. I remembered chicken wings dripping in buffalo sauce and greasy pizza and that less than three months later I left Shermantown to become a wrestler.

"I kept tabs on you," Dylan said.

The waitress dropped off my black coffee, Dylan's Coke. She was thin, pimple-faced. Not far out of high school herself, I'd guess. She wrote our orders verbatim in her notepad, none of the bravado of more seasoned waitresses who assured customers they'd remember everything. I preferred the studious type, the record keepers. They never got the order wrong.

"I'd search your name on the Internet—try to keep track of all your gimmicks. And when YouTube came out, I got to see some of your matches."

He'd bought copies of the first VHS tapes and DVDs I had matches on. Low-res, low-quality stuff, where I was curtain jerking or working bathroom break matches in the middle of the card. The promoters got mad when YouTube became a thing—people putting up matches for free, the writing on the wall that tape revenue was going to be a thing of the past. I was happy about it, though. A lot of us were. Convinced ourselves that being on the Internet was as good as being on TV where anyone might find our matches, where we might be discovered.

"I remember the first time. You were wearing these purple pants and a gold top."

I remembered that era. That persona. I played a gypsy-type, long before anyone thought to call a term like that culturally insensitive. I did an approximation of a belly dance on my way to the ring, except I'd never learned to belly dance—I'm not sure I'd ever even seen one—so I did the best that my boyfriend at the time and I could come up with. I thought it was sort of sexy then, but when I've looked back at footage it proved even more embarrassing than I'd feared.

I'd get five minutes—if I was lucky with a veteran, but often as not with a girl as green as I was. Usually prettier than me. It didn't take long to settle into my role as a solid hand who could make girls who barely trained look a lot better than they were. I still rushed, though. Trying to get all my spots in—always something off the top rope—before the veterans got through about slowing down. About how less is more and how every wrestler has a bump card—a number of falls to the canvas they can take before their body gives out and they'll have to retire. No one knows how many bumps they have in them, but a bump off the top rope sure as hell counted for three or four holes punched from the card.

"I couldn't believe it, watching you. I know we messed around in the tennis court and you were a daredevil. But here you are, really *doing it*—dropkicks and hurricanranas and moonsaults." He shook his head in wonder. "And then on TV I see Randy Orton chinlocking somebody to sleep—not just the wrestler, but the audience too. It's such a snoozefest. They call those rest holds right? So both guys can catch their breath?"

The waitress was back she left my egg-white omelette, his Belgian waffle covered in powdered sugar, surrounded by a ring of whipped cream and halved strawberries, a square of butter melting on top. He slathered it all in maple syrup.

The idea of rest holds got out on the Internet—that a chinlock, a bearhug, a full nelson were designed to let the wrestlers both relax for a minute and gather their strength for another flurry of action. It's not untrue, but there are other reasons, like letting the crowd settle so they'll pop for the next big move. "There's a difference between TV wrestling and what you see in the arena." I cut into my omelette. There was too much cheese on it, so I scraped some to the side. "If you're on TV, there are broadcasters and a lot of fans don't realize they're telling half the story—telling you how to feel. The TV wrestlers grab a hold and they're giving the color commentator the chance to the tell story behind the match, about how this body part has been injured for years or about what a technician one guy is or why this hold is so dangerous it's been banned in sixteen states."

I laughed at myself a little at that last part, because it was absurd, but I did know a commentator once, coming down from the big leagues to record the vocal track over our big show the promoter was going to sell on DVD, and he made a big deal out of holds that were banned or illegal in amateur wrestling because of the risk of causing so much pain they could cause a psychological break. It was all make-believe. One of the nights he showed up drunk and wound up laughing at himself. The promoter canned him and scrapped the whole DVD project because it would cost too much to rerecord the commentary. A lot of the boys in the locker room were mad because they were counting on the DVD royalties and it took everything I had in me not to laugh at them. Hang around this business long enough, and you know there aren't any DVD royalties coming your way—even if the DVD does come to fruition and does sell enough copies to make up production costs (not to mention how improbable those propositions were). Promoters were charlatans and grifters. The best you could count on was the money they promised you the night you wrestled, and even then *the gate wasn't quite what we expected* or *the arena hit me with a fee to use their lighting guy, so I'm a little light.* Always, *I'll make it up to you at the next town.*

Dylan was starry-eyed, a little whipped cream on his lower lip. He had crow's feet at the corners of his eyes and some gray in his hair, but in a moment like this I could see the teenager in him again.

I wanted to tell him I've been in a thousand diners like this, a thousand late nights. I watched Bruiser Magee eat a dozen eggs, twenty strips of bacon and chase it all down with two pots of coffee. I was there when Lelah Dorengo and seven-foot-tall Potter Hoytes disappeared to the ladies' room together and locked themselves inside and the whole diner could hear what they were up to minutes before a waitress, then the manager caught on, beating on the door. Lelah and Potter didn't rush themselves, but when they were done, Potter opened the door and came out casually, stood chest to face with the manager and dared him to say something more about how he was going to call the police; the manager said nothing. I was there when Johnny Flex got into it with Wheelbarrow Willy because he thought he'd slept with his girl and there was the night Sissy Folgers called me out to the parking lot because she was high and thought I'd been too stiff with her in the ring that night. I stepped outside and body slammed her into the windshield of a Corolla. Next thing I knew, someone was throwing me in the backseat of a car and peeling out before the police arrived, car alarm wailing into the night.

All these diners, all these nights, all these stories I could tell. But I never experienced what Dylan did a couple minutes later, midway through showing me a photo of Malcolm holding his little sister Missy, when a text notification showed up. First name only. Wendy.

He turned the phone away to read the full message, then text something back. He was still typing when he started talking to me again. "I love my kids. I love my wife. I love my life." He paused, tapping a couple times more on the screen before the phone made a *whoosh* sound of a text going out. "But I don't think I'll ever get rid of that part of me that regrets not hitting the road with you. I could've been a wrestler too. Can you imagine that? Had that whole life?"

I heard the regrets of a life not lived. I'd heard it before from a hundred fans who hung around for autographs after shows. And there was the obvious corollary, as he turned back to showing me pictures of Malcolm grown up and his daughter Missy and of the professional photos they had done at an orchard last autumn that maybe I, too, missed out on something when I chose wrestling, moving territory to territory. Didn't I wish I'd stayed home and built a life like his?

Every opportunity chosen is the choice to regret another thing. Dylan's phone vibrated in his hand. Another text from Wendy.

She called him home, of course. Asked how much later he'd be out. Reminded him the kids had school in the morning and he had work and she missed him and hoped she'd get to see him before she went to sleep and she hoped he didn't get too carried away having late-night breakfast with his high school sweetheart and making the kind of choices he would have in high school and he'd regret by the light of day. Something like that.

Dylan looked sheepish. Like a younger version of himself I'd once known whose mom told him he had to visit his grandmother on Sunday when he and I had plans to go to the mall. "It looks like I'm going to turn into a pumpkin." He tipped back his Coke, foregoing the straw, drinking down the dregs, sliding a half-melted ice chip into his mouth. "It was good to see you."

"You too."

We haggled over who'd pick up the bill (I paid, he tipped). I got up first. We walked out together. He held the door for me. We hugged outside. We'd parked our cars on opposite ends of the lot.

The speakers spat static after I'd turned on my Civic. I'd forgotten that I lost signal more and more as I'd traveled north on the turnpike. I'd turned the dial for a while but got preoccupied as I drew closer to my destination. I turned down the volume there in the parking lot before I put the car into reverse to pull out, then put it in drive to pull away.

Lights flashed. Dylan offering one last goodbye as I drove past. I didn't bother to stop or even look. We'd said enough goodbyes already.

It took a beat longer to realize I hadn't turned my headlights on. It might not have been Dylan, but anyone at all pointing out that I was driving out into the dark and no one could see me coming.

I turned my lights on.

Dylan was heading home.

I was heading onward.

WEDLOCK

The conventional wisdom in wrestling locker rooms is this: you don't shit where you eat.

Early in my career Lady Mayhem laid it out for me while she applied her face paint in a magnetized little mirror she affixed to lockers from town to town. That night she went for a crescent of silver over one eye, a crescent of purple over the other. "Men in this business don't want to be a part of some great romance. They want sex and they want somebody to take care of them."

In Lady Mayhem's day, men kept women in different towns and called them ring rats. Yes, it was about sex. But the older guys were practical about it, too. They cultivated different relationships in different towns to have someone who'd pick them up from an airport, let them crash in their bed, make them a home-cooked meal, do their laundry as they passed through.

The times changed. Nowadays, there's STD awareness and cautionary tales about paying child support across state lines. That, and there are more women on most wrestling promotions' payrolls, playing more than eye candy roles, ready to put men in their place if they use the *rat* word.

Still, I understand what Lady Mayhem was telling me about not getting mixed up with another wrestler. On a long enough timetable, it's not a question of if, but when any relationship will go sour. There's having to see your ex in the workplace, and then there's having to see your ex, sweating in spandex in the workplace night after night. That's not to mention the jealousy if one partner's star takes off and the other's doesn't, besides the ramifications if somebody gets cut from the roster, or someone gets a better opportunity to wrestle elsewhere.

But Ethan Adams and I talked about choice. About how things would only go sour if we chose for them to, and we liked one another a lot, and why not mutually agree that even if we broke up in the end, we'd still like one another forever?

We talked late at night on the hood of the beater convertible he drove from town to town, eating vanilla soft serve from a twenty-four-hour burger joint. We were the only ones in the parking lot and it was humid and the ice cream was sweet. He held my hand under the glow of a neon sign that read *Come on in and have a taste!*

The moment Ethan climbed on top of me and locked lips I put aside everything Lady Mayhem had ever told me.

#

Ethan and I moved fast. I guess that's another reason why people say not to date in the locker room. For all the stereotypes about wrestlers being brutes, a lot of us are romantics, all too ready to get swept up.

Ethan proposed. No grand gesture, no pomp and circumstance, no ring. We were both spendthrifts in the tradition of the business, and he knew I'd clean his clock if he spent hundreds, let alone thousands of dollars on jewelry. In the flicker of a tube television, a crumby motel in between towns, sitting on top of a coffee-stained comforter, he asked me if I wanted to.

So we got hitched. Little fanfare. My mother was dead and most of my friends were wrestlers working across the country, overseas, who could keep track of them? Ethan was different. Had a big family that he said would want to be there if he ever got married, but we eloped anyway. Manny Hill, a legend, worked a spot appearance for a big show. When he talked backstage about how Jesus had saved him and he'd become a reverend, we took it for the half-baked sign we wanted it to be and asked if he'd officiate our ceremony that night. In Ethan's vows, he talked about choice—that theme we'd founded our relationship on—and how we'd choose one another day. And though, in my mind, I saw the specter of Lady Mayhem shaking her head, I told him plain and simple that I chose him before I said, "I do."

\#

Maybe I should've resented it when the booker put me and Ethan into a mixed tag team. Did our coupling have to mean that our wrestling fates would be intertwined, too? Would working, not only out of the same locker room, but in the same matches night after night fray our marriage?

The thing is that it worked. Both of us were doing fine, but our characters didn't have much direction. Insert an angle when Ethan got beat down by Great Eight faction— a cluster of four male and four female heels—and I came to his aid, not to cover his body like the loyal, docile damsel, but swinging a steel folding chair to smash anything that moved. The moment paved the way for me and Ethan's wrestling fates to come together. It also gave us a wide permutation of male and female partners to butt heads with over the months to follow.

We developed our own tandem hold, born out of Ethan already using an ankle lock and half crab combo as his finisher. He'd apply his hold, then I'd grab the victim's other ankle and twist it and wrench the leg back to effectively double the pain. We called it the Wedlock. Despite the questionable legality in tag team wrestling rules of us both being in the ring for that double team, we tended to use it in the heat of a fray when all four participants were in action, when it was difficult to tell who was legal anymore. The referee couldn't be blamed for shrugging his shoulders and counting the submission.

We always got the submission when we used Wedlock. It might've killed the credibility of Ethan's hold for it not to have gotten the job done with the two of us using it at the same time, both for the pain and the inability to power out of two wrestlers clamping on simultaneously like that. New York Nick Nettles sold it best, pushing up on his triceps, arching his back and screaming out into the crowd before a tearful surrender.

Ethan talked about our hold when we cut promos. Ring announcer Charlie Folks wedged between us, angling the microphone up toward Ethan's mouth, looking something like a wedding officiant in his bedazzled tuxedo, in between us in our matching black and white wrestling gear.

"There's nothing more painful than Wedlock," Ethan said. "There's not a man alive who can withstand it."

\#

Not every wrestling marriage goes the distance. Hell, it's a cliche that most don't because how are two people who fight for a living going to talk out their problems in the long term? Marriages fall apart behind the scenes, though. Wrestlers, at least on the big stage, have to be professionals and leave their business away from the cameras and the live crowds. Unless you're Kevin and Nancy Sullivan.

Lady Mayhem would remind any young woman getting swept up in a wrestling romance about the Sullivans. Kevin doubled as not only wrestler, but head writer, and booked an angle for Nancy to leave him for the younger, better-looking Chris Benoit.

"Kevin told them to travel together," Lady Mayhem said. "He wanted people to see them hold hands in public and whisper sweet nothings over cocktails at airport bars. This is before the Internet or Twitter. He thought if enough people saw them, word of mouth would catch on and all the fans would buy into the story."

Maybe Kevin was too confident in his marriage to imagine Nancy leaving him. Maybe he saw the writing was on the wall that Nancy and Chris were falling in love in real life and put his feelings aside for the sake of the story. Regardless of what he knew or intended, the part that's not up for debate is that he wrote the demise of his own marriage. Lady Mayhem spelled out the moral in case anyone missed it, that even the wrestler with the greater experience, the greater influence, the greater power could get burned.

The storyline ended. Nancy stayed with Chris on screen and off. They had a son together.

\#

Me and Ethan didn't waste time getting pregnant. I'd cleared forty and Ethan was committed to having at least one biological child.

We got lucky, it all happened so fast.

But it didn't feel lucky. Because the moment I got pregnant was the moment I started mourning everything I'd lose. The margaritas I couldn't partake in at the Mexican restaurant that night were the first thing to hit me, inconsequential as they were. That night, lying in bed, the knowledge that I wouldn't wrestle again for easily a year—forty weeks of pregnancy, then time for my body to heal, not to mention the question of who'd watch the baby if I went back on the road. I didn't see Ethan sitting out long. We weren't close to our families.

"Our son'll travel," Ethan reassured me. "A road warrior from day one."

I wasn't sure that's how it worked.

I wasn't sure we'd have a son.

The ultrasound confirmed I was carrying a boy, though. It was funny what a reassurance it felt like, not because I favored a boy but because I knew Ethan expected one, had only wrapped his head around being a father so far as raising a son went. He'd never given reason for me to doubt he'd be the father to whatever child we had, but that's part of mothering, isn't it? To worry. To nest in those early stages and insist we needed to stop renting because we needed a stable home, and so we bought a little house, painted the nursery walls baby blue, and assembled a crib and collected a rocking chair, a changing table, baby bottles, a swing.

The booker stopped by our house. A nice gesture. He brought a pea green teddy bear and told me my spot would be waiting for me when I got back. He had ideas for a heel turn, for me to be bitter about everyone forgetting me, about no one coming to see me after the baby shower. Maybe I'd join the Great Eight. Someone from the faction would probably have moved on from the territory by then, or if not, would be overdue for a face turn to freshen the story. I'd take their spot.

I held the bear tight to my stomach, over where the baby bump would be, though I wasn't showing yet. I tried to believe him about my spot, about future plans, as if life would go on the way I'd known it and everything—anything—would be the same.

I worked one more show before I was off TV. One last Wedlock on Bull Barrymore, after Ethan had done the heavy lifting chasing off the rest of The Great Eight. I was in for the hold, delivering the justice in one last feel-good moment where my body didn't absorb any punishment.

Then I was gone.

\#

One of the last times Lady Mayhem and I talked, before her fourth stab at a retirement, and when I was on my way out of town for a run back east, she went over more of the Nancy Sullivan story with me. The second act: after she and Kevin were done, after she'd remarried to Chris Benoit and took his name and had his child.

"His son Daniel was seven years old." Lady Mayhem looked genuinely sad when she remembered that part, though I may have only interpreted sadness into her exhausted form, after she'd been put through an announce table at the end of a hardcore match she was too old to have been working. "Nancy was off the road, raising him. Chris's hard work paid off, too, finally winning a world title. They had confetti drop from the ceiling and everything for him."

The wife, the kid, the championship. Make a movie and this is when the credits roll.

But Chris Benoit wasn't a stage name. It was his real one. A real man whose story went on until he really murdered his wife and son.

Blame it on an argument gone too far. Or 'roid rage. "In the end, everyone seemed to blame it on concussions warping his mind," Lady Mayhem explained.

He killed Nancy first.

Daniel second, with bruising that suggested Chris used a variation of his Crippler Crossface hold to do the deed, his signature finisher from the wrestling ring, after sedating the boy with Xanax. Chris then hung himself from a weight machine in his home gym.

I already knew the story in broad strokes. That Benoit was a monster, first and foremost for what he did, but secondarily because he put a stain on the business—wasn't professional wrestling stigmatized enough without a woman and child killer?

Years later, Ethan on the road, me at home and pregnant, with nothing but time to think, I tried to envision the Benoits. Imagine an argument gone off the rails into physical violence. Chris's revelation that he'd killed his wife and his life was over—his choices: prison, the death sentence, or offing himself. And what about the son left behind, understanding little but that his mother was dead and his father was to blame and who in the world could he ever trust again?

I imagined anyone might have a breakdown. I imagined Ethan coming off the road in a bad mood.

\#

We named our son Miles, after the miles traveled on the road, so integral to our identities as wrestlers—more than a job, a way of life.

Ethan didn't make it home for the birth, even though I was overdue and suggested he should get off the road until the kid came. Ethan was a wrestler through and through, never wanting to miss a date. "Besides," he said, "we need the money."

We did need the money, because the crap private insurance we'd bought together only covered some of the hospital bills. The reality had set in that we'd have thousands of dollars of debt coming our way. But more than that, I'd needed Ethan. No family to be seen, I held Miles in the hospital until I fell asleep. The nurses caught me and said that wasn't safe and I needed to put him in the bassinet.

Miles was quiet for the better part of a day.

Then he exploded.

He was always hungry. Or cold. Or lonely. Or overwhelmed with this world of bright lights and air and infinite space. I cried with him.

He suckled at my breast. The nurses said he was a good eater. Some babies struggled to latch and some mothers couldn't produce enough milk to keep up with the demand, but the two of us were off to a good start.

He lost weight. Came out seven pounds, went down to six, bounced back up to six and a half. They told me this was good, too. It took time for a breastfed baby to grow.

Ethan got to the hospital and nodded along as I tried to catch him up to speed. I'm not sure he listened to a word. He was in love with our boy, I'll give him that much. He never took his eyes off him.

When the nurses said it was time to go, I said it couldn't be. I was supposed to have two nights. They said I had been there two nights, and I wondered if it were possible that much time had disappeared. I knew I'd drifted off a few times, maybe for a couple hours total. I knew it had felt like an eternity before Ethan got there.

Ethan got Miles in the car seat. Miles didn't look comfortable and I asked one of the nurses to look, and she pointed out the straps were too tight and showed us the lever to hold down to loosen them, and that we might want to adjust the height of the headrest. I hadn't realized there was so much to get wrong.

\#

I was exhausted before Ethan left. Even after he learned how to change a diaper and pitched in, after he did a couple loads of laundry. There was too much, and then he was back on the road to make his next spot.

And Miles and I were alone.

There's a sense of feeling physically drained any wrestler knows full well, when your legs are jelly and it hurts to lift your arms enough to so much as put a shirt on a hanger, and your back aches. You ice and you sleep as long as you can, before it's back to the gym, back to the ring, on to the next town.

I couldn't shake the exhaustion those first weeks of motherhood, between the intermittent sleep and never-ending stream of feedings and rocking and diaper changes and baths. There was no rush of adrenaline from the roar of a live crowd. No commiserating in the locker room about fatigue and chronic pain.

I found a livestream of Ethan wrestling, but Miles cried over it too loudly.

\#

I thought I might murder Ethan when he came back. Because he didn't pick up Miles right away. *What kind of father was he?* Then, because he held Miles too long. *Was he trying to take him from me?*

He gave me Miles when the boy wouldn't stop crying. The baby was calmer in my arms. There was some pleasure in that. Knowing that I was this boy's favorite, just as he was mine, even if that was only by process of elimination because we were usually the only people in one another's lives.

\#

Months passed.

\#

When Ethan was home for a longer stretch, I entered a rage because I caught him using the old sponge I used to wipe the counters to wash Ethan's bottle, all that grease and grime and salmonella seeping into the plastic in soapy suds. In addition, he'd piled all the dishes he'd washed with that sponge into the drying rack on top of the clean dishes that were already there. I'd have to wash everything again.

I hit Ethan hard against the chest and fell to my knees and sobbed. When I looked back, Miles was there, oblivious, kicking at the ceiling. He was capable of rolling over by then and moving at more of a slither than a crawl but was mostly content to lie on his back and think.

In a calmer space, I told Ethan I was worried about myself.

My fears of him coming back and pulling a Chris Benoit had long ago dissipated, because if anything he was too cavalier—not stressed or overwhelmed but more like the doofus uncle who swooped in on intervals to take the kid off my hands for a couple hours, which would have been fine if there'd been a father in the picture, too.

I told him I was worried *I'd* play Chris Benoit in our family's story, losing my cool one day and hurting, maybe killing Ethan, and then what would become of Miles?

And Ethan reminded me about choice.

That he could choose to be more present, and he would—that he knew he hadn't been around as much as he wanted to. But that I had a choice, too. Not that I didn't have a right to get mad, but I'd never be a monster like Benoit if I kept making the conscious choice not to.

Hadn't Lady Mayhem said something like that, too? That difference between Benoit and any other wrestler was that he hadn't stopped himself. That he was more monster than man in those final moments.

\#

Years passed.

\#

I don't know that Ethan was right about choice.

Because where was the line between a choice and acting on instinct?

As wrestlers, weren't acts of violence more instinctive to us? Or was the inverse true? As wrestlers, we knew how to hit and be hit, but we were also trained to keep one another safe.

Ethan and I would have our disagreements, not least of all when I started Miles's wrestling training, such as it was, at five years old. I taught him the basics like how to lock up, how to grab a headlock, how to fall with as much surface area of his body as possible hitting the floor to distribute the impact and protect himself from hurt.

There are two kinds of wrestlers who are fathers—the ones obsessed with children following in their footsteps and the ones who will do anything to stop it. Ethan didn't want Miles following us into wresting. He said he wanted a better life for him in that abstract way wrestlers talk about college and office jobs as if they are superior.

After Ethan told me to stop, after Miles begged me to keep going, I made the boy promise this would be our secret from his father. When he agreed, I focused less on wrestling performance and more on transferable skills like how to take a punch and how to give one, the knowledge that would protect him on the schoolyard as a kid, at some bar on a Saturday night as a man.

And I chose to get back in the ring.

Call it a comeback. Call it a farewell tour. Truth be told, I wasn't certain which it was. Only that I'd made the choice to get in the ring again that summer before Miles started kindergarten. The boy came on the road with me.

With us.

The booker was good to his word and let me come back. The Great Eight had dissolved a year and a half earlier. The fan base had changed too. I was reintroduced as a grizzled veteran, bitter about the pretty young girls fans gravitated to. Still hungry after all of those years for a taste of what was rightfully mine.

That first explosion of skin on skin, Heidi Chabon popped me good in the cheek—harder than I think she meant to—I knew I was back where I belonged.

The way my back ached after I'd suplexed her, I figured my body wasn't long for the wrestling world.

But Ethan was waiting at the curtain. I didn't realize he'd let Miles watch the whole match from there. Afterward, the kid hugged my leg tight, and Ethan kissed me hard and wet, a dry arm over my sweat-soaked shoulders. I apologized and told them both I was a stinking mess, but they didn't let go.

DESTINATION

The thing about kids is they grow up. The thing about marriages is they end. The thing about wrestlers is they never retire. I learned that before my career began. I'd become an old wrestler—one of the things I'd promised myself I'd never be. I'd already broken most of the other promises.

Out on my own again, I had a destination. Get to Ravenscroft in British Columbia, fifty miles shy of Yukon. Maybe it was my introduction to Canadian hospitality that I was told to get there when I could.

I saw redwoods and drank at wineries, racking up credit card charges at gas stations, the occasional motel, a cider house in Oregon, a doughnut shop that I didn't realize was across the border of Washington state until a local told me so.

There was a line at the Canadian border. A man in the lane to the left of me held up a cardboard half of a smile to the drivers he crossed paths with out his window. I told myself the story that this man crossed this border on the regular, such that he came prepared with this nicety. Something to amuse children. Something for tourists to take a picture of at this otherwise slow, joyless leg of their vacation. Something to brighten somebody's day, prompt a smile of their own in response to the absurdity of this artificial one, if just for a moment. That I stonewalled him, only watching out of my peripheral vision and fixing my gaze straight ahead, must have egged him on. At a particular standstill, both of our lanes stopped for several minutes, he unfastened his safety belt, rolled down the passenger side window and leaned his long torso out, stretched his arm and tapped on my window.

The cardboard smile.

I stretched my thumb and drew it slow and steady across my throat, the universal signal I will *kill kill kill* you in cold blood.

He turned pale. I waited until I'd driven far enough ahead that there was no chance he could see to smile.

#

I drove through wooded roads with narrow shoulders, nowhere at all to pull off, no choice but to carry on driving past a bursting bladder, fighting off sleep.

I drove until I got to Ravenscroft, just in time, according Wooly Franklin III.

In the tradition of the business, Wooly Franklin Sr., like The Emperor in Damphry, like Machete Betty in Motor City, was a wrestler and a promoter. A man like that booked himself on top as long as he could go because he'd learned early that you couldn't trust just anybody in the wrestling business. You could trust yourself not to leave, not to hold yourself up for money, not to become a pain in the ass questioning your creative.

Which came first, the nickname Wooly or the bushy beard that had to have been dyed black by then? He'd wrestled across four decades before mostly hanging up his boots, though the boys said he still carried a duffel bag to each show with tights and knee pads just in case.

But now he focused his attention backstage, left the wrestling to the next generation. Never mind that Wooly wasn't the promoter's real name—his eldest son was Wooly Jr. just the same. He mostly tag teamed with Walter, the youngest of the brood, whose lazy eye duped folks into thinking he was simple—and his wrestling persona was—but he was actually the most bookish of the bunch and generally agreed to be the most likely to one day take over his father's business. There was Padric, the best looking with his square jaw and chiseled physique, who spent most of his time as champion or in the title hunt. And there was Lucy, the lone girl. Scraggly. Bespectacled backstage, she hit the ring half-blind without her glasses. That didn't stop her from slinging opponents across the ring with suplexes and diving at them from the top rope.

Lucy was my first opponent.

Wooly the third, whom the boys called The Turd, who'd been backstage since he was in diapers, who was Wooly Jr.'s son but whom by all indications Lucy had done most of the raising of, who was twelve and looked more like he was ten and everyone agreed would be wrestling by the time he was fifteen—he warned me to watch for Lucy's discus punch.

"She can't see good enough to land it right," he said. "So just lean in and sell it hard and don't get caught unawares."

From what I could gather, Lucy was ten-to-fifteen years younger than me, and proportionally less experienced. Ordinarily, that meant a wrestler would defer to the veteran by way of seniority and let me call the action in the ring. She was Wooly's daughter, though, besides which she wasn't just half-blind but half-deaf so she directed traffic if only because she couldn't be directed.

We worked well enough together. Anyone with the Franklin surname was a fan favorite across the Canadian Cross Country Circuit cities, so I heeled it up with a bag of hair pulling and eye gouging tricks.

Lucy called for the discus, and I did what the kid said, swaying into the path of her fist and acting like I got cold-cocked as she breezed by.

She pulled me up by a handful of hair, muttering the next instructions in that way veterans can do, made to look like she was telling me how much she hated me when the words that came out were, *Irish whip, back drop, kick, catch, enzuguiri.* A basic enough sequence in practice, but enough words for a less experienced performer to get lost. I'd earned her trust in the preceding minutes that I was a serious and skilled worker, not deadweight for her carry—a fair concern for anyone new to the territory, but particularly women because pretty faces often got a pass, and because of that there was a low bar remaining for whom could be called skilled worker.

As she backed me into the ropes, I remembered a sensation I must've felt a dozen, maybe a hundred times before by then. Maybe I could find my place, settle in with this promotion. Carve out a life.

I bounced off the far ropes and ran to Lucy's poised form, ready to swing up my right leg, light but fast, minimize impact, let her catch it, but still make it look good. I'd hop on my left foot, then, once the crowd was certain she had me, leap, swing that left foot up to nail the side of her head and take over.

Maybe I was too fast, getting too close too soon. Maybe I was too slow and Lucy had thought I'd messed up the spot. Regardless, when I got close, she swung her head up with a vengeance, the back of her skull to my teeth. We were both hurt, as she stumbled, clutching her head, and I was conscious of my mouth bleeding, a throbbing pain from just above my jaw. I tried to swallow and choked, spitting blood on the mat until I hacked loose the tooth that had slid down my throat.

My tooth. What I'd learn afterward from Walter was called a central incisor.

Lucy didn't call the next move, but caught a bearhug around my torso, then threw me overhead, bridging her body to pin me in a Northern Lights Suplex. The referee had already counted two when I remembered this was her finisher, and the conclusion we'd meant to come to, but after I'd worked a heat segment on her and after she'd gotten some shine on her comeback. She'd decided that we would go home early, and I wasn't in any position to argue.

And just as quickly as I thought I might find a place with CCCC, I felt certain I'd blown my opportunity that first night. It may have been Lucy's fault—at least as much as mine—how things had broken down, but she was the boss's daughter, and it was my first night on the job.

I lost track of the tooth in those moments to follow and was backstage before I thought to recover it, the next set of wrestlers already on their way to the ring.

Lucy came to me backstage. "Fuck it, sorry I got you, lass." Lucy'd spent a couple year stint in Ireland as a teenager, a compromise between sending her to college—where she'd made clear her greatest desire was to study abroad—and go into the wrestling business as her siblings had been instinctively drawn to do. She'd come back with the lilt of an Irish accent on her voice—mostly gone by the time I got there, though it still resurfaced sometimes when she drank Irish whisky. That and a few choice words, like *gammy* to describe her brothers when they were drunk, or *feek* to describe beautiful women, to undermine that they had any talent. *They're just feeks* who got on the card without having to work for it, and whom she'd have to babysit from bell to bell.

Get her drinking, and Lucy would explain to anyone who'd listen, no matter how many times they'd heard it, that people in Ireland didn't really say *lass*, it was a stereotype, and yet as if to force the contradiction, as if to dare a confrontation, she'd go on using it herself.

I was still learning Lucy then, though those moments backstage suggested that she liked me well enough. After one match, she was ready to talk to me like a colleague, ready, even, to admit that she'd botched the backdrop-kick spot.

I told her it was all right.

If I weren't in the haze of a new territory, only getting settled so far as meeting the locker room before we all hit the road for the next show, four hundred miles away, I might have tended to my tooth—looked more purposefully for the one that had been knocked out or assessed the possibility of an implant. But I let it go, joining no shortage of others in the CCCC locker room who were missing a tooth or two, whose noses were permanently bent for resetting them themselves after they got busted, who walked with permanent limps and whose hands were bent into claws easier to ball into a fist than to stretch wide.

I drove behind Lucy, Wooly Jr., and The Turd, following their taillights along dark roads until I couldn't even see road until I saw a sign warning about the prospective dangers of driving over a frozen lake. We went by it too fast to read it carefully. I turned down my heater a couple notches and lowered the window, on the hopes of better hearing a cracking sound should one emerge from beneath the car. As if I had somewhere to turn off. As if I had any choice but to keep barreling forward.

I lost hours on that drive. The pain in my mouth, the rush coming off a show, the constant pressure on the gas pedal to keep up with my guides lest I get lost forever in the Canadian wilderness. Look at the clock once and it was midnight. Pull off for gas and it was three in the morning. Drive on, coffee steaming in my cup holder, but going too fast around too many bends to dare drink from it. Look again and day was breaking.

And we'd arrived.

We arrived at a lodge where we stayed and ate free in exchange for tickets to the show, in exchange for the proprietor being able to advertise that we stayed to draw in more customers for the privilege of eating next to, sleeping next to, breathing the same air as the wrestlers. I was ready to get to my room and sleep until it was time to go to the arena, but Lucy put an arm over me and guided me toward the dining commons instead.

There were long wooden tables all in rows, set up a feast. The lodge staff brought heaping platters of eggs and bacon and buttery rolls for us to help ourselves from, coffee mugs the size of sauce pans. A reassurance to *just give a holler* when we needed refills.

The food was hot and good, and it occurred to me it'd been days since I'd had a proper meal of more than candy bars, potato chips, energy drinks, and bottled water on the road. My mid-section had gone soft enough I was embarrassed to be seen in the ring the night before with Lucy—had it only been one night? But here, we ate well, not the first wrestlers to arrive, but far from the last as we ate and ate and ate.

Belly full, head swimming with stories of the CCCC and the Franklin family—inevitably intersecting with one another—I was ready for sleep. For all of the coffee I'd downed—strong enough that I could almost chew it—I might've been roused, but rather I recognized it as the only thing keeping me up, its gentle buzz succumbing by degrees to the throb in the front of my skull. My bladder felt ready to burst.

The bathroom at the dining commons was putrid— just a single toilet and sink, a roll where paper towels might hang. The toilet seat was splattered with a mixture of rust-colored stains and fresher drops of moisture, the smell of rot in the air. I squatted, hovering inches above the seat. As a wrestler, I'd learned not to worry much about what was sanitary, with the knowledge I'd roll around on the mats with other women, with men and their stinking bodies and there was always a shower on the other end, no logical reason to try to stay clean. But there were limits.

When I left the bathroom, Wooly and the Turd were waiting for me. The family elder had a hand on his youngest relation's shoulder in what looked like more or less equally a protective stance and like the old man were using the boy like a cane to prop up a body that was brittle at its joints, too heavy around the middle.

"I have an arrangement for you," Wooly said.

I was no stranger to the principle of rookies being assigned tasks by locker room veterans, and I could tell from something in Wooly's posture and tone of voice that an assignment was on its way. Oftentimes, these tasks were along the lines of carrying an old timer's bags, gassing up the boss's car in the early morning, or helping to take down the ring after a show. I'd wrestled for years by then but wasn't a big enough star for my credits from other territories to transfer here. Here, I was still new blood, and I still needed to prove myself.

"You're going to ride with Turd."

The more traditional territories insisted that faces and heels not co-mingle. Past that, most wrestlers were left to their own devices in deciding who to share cars with. Those times when someone was assigned, it was typically a matter of one wrestler babysitting the other who had a drug problem or trouble making it to the arenas on time or needed someone to nudge him into finding time to get to gym between towns to keep up his muscular physique.

"I figure you might learn a thing or two from one another," Wooly went on. "You're a good hand and can get the boy here ready for when it's time to hit the mat himself in a few years. And he can tell you who's who and which town is which while you're getting acclimated."

It was literal babysitting and absurd when the kid's own brothers and sister were on the road, too. I might have made a stink out of getting tasked with childcare on account of being a woman, but then wasn't there something to be said for Wooly trusting me with his youngest son at all?

I might have argued the point had Turd looked scared. But on the contrary, he looked all too eager, smart enough to recognize his siblings had grown tired of him and thirsting at the prospect of distilling all he'd come to know about CCCC to someone who might listen.

"Turd's got our room key already," Wooly said. "Maybe he'll let you get some shut-eye before you head to the arena." He added, as it if were an afterthought, "Turd knows the way."

\#

Turd did know the way to our room after a glance at the key. Second floor. He left his suitcase for me to lug without asking, without apology, and sped ahead up the cement stairs. It was bitter cold out, the stairs mercifully covered so that no snow or ice layered onto them.

In the room, I flopped down on the bed. I think I must have slept, though not for long. Minutes? Seconds? Long enough for the flicker of a dream. Long enough to be convinced I was home and Mom scolded me for not tending to the stove, for letting scrambled eggs burn, and I pled with her that they weren't my eggs, that Dad must have started them, then fallen asleep on his recliner. She wouldn't listen. *This is all your fault.* Still, she didn't tend to the eggs, letting them char and smoke. *All your fault.*

I woke to that smell of burning.

The smoke detector hung loose from the wall. There was a chair beneath it that I quickly understood Turd had climbed on to disable the alarm, foreseeing the smoke.

The ironing board was set up, the iron was plugged into the wall. A cake of dry Ramen noodles burning.

I was up.

I asked what he was doing, grabbed a hand towel from the bathroom to scoop up the noodles, threw them in the sink, and ran water over them. Turd said he was trying to a new way of making Ramen, fried. I asked how he could possibly be hungry.

He told me he wasn't hungry.

He was curious.

He was curious, too, about whether, if he flipped back and forth between TV stations, if the programs might merge, layering on top of one another and playing simultaneously in the liminal space between them. He was curious about whether a towel that was completely soaked through would take longer to dry on the rack than one that was merely wetted all around, and if hot or cold water would make any difference. (This was how he made his way through all four bath towels the housekeeping staff had provided the room.)

I addressed each of Turd's trials after enough time, enough noise, enough annoyance, returning to bed, folding the pillow over my head, trying to sleep, even succeeding once or twice, but after a while, it wasn't even that I was stirred by what he was doing as much as I was by the fear for what he *might* do unsupervised in that hotel room. Maybe he felt liberated from the stricter eyes of his siblings. Maybe this was all a continuation, tending to curiosities he hadn't addressed yet, or ones spawned by previous experiences.

I told him I was going to shower. I told him he needed to stay in the chair and watch television, and that he could only turn the television station a maximum of three times, and could not turn the volume up, only down. He nodded and asked if he could turn the television on and off. (No.) If he could adjust the settings like brightness and tint. (Yes.) If he could play with closed captioning. (Yes.) If he could charge a movie to the room. (No.)

His questions exhausted, I showered quickly, not waiting for the water to warm. I couldn't leave him alone too long, besides which I needed to wake up. The cold water was good for that. The hotel soap smelled of maple. I wrapped the dryest towel I could find around my torso on the way out, applied the next driest to my hair.

Remarkably enough, Turd was in his chair, with the television on, but the volume turned all the way down, the brightness turned dim as low as it would go. He was writing on a hotel notepad, not watching TV, and I asked him why he hadn't turned it off, and he told me I'd said he couldn't. I asked him what he was writing. He told me it was a story about dragons and proceeded to read aloud while I got dressed, then tell the rest of the story extemporaneously. I couldn't hear him over the sweet reprieve of the blow dryer.

Turd navigated us to the arena, where we were early, where only his family was there going over notes for the show, the creative plans coming out of it. A couple of broad-backed trainees arrived after us, charged with setting up the ring and the railing around it that would separate the fans from the talents. No one seemed surprised that Turd and I were there ahead of the bulk of the roster.

"You lasted a while at the hotel with him." Walter offered a smile. "I'm impressed."

#

Turd found the CD binder stuffed beneath my car seat, a relic I'd all but forgotten was there, only occasionally, passively thinking of along my longest drives. I never thought to fish it out when I stopped for gas or food or sleep.

But Turd was a kid and needed space to move along our long rides so he rode in the back and paced and crawled through the space as if it were much more expansive than it was, and who knows what imaginary worlds he created for himself when he'd leap from one side to another, hard enough to make the car shake and make me worry about the suspension. Maybe he was dreaming of a cross-body block off the second ropes. Just as likely, it was a saving-the-princess-from-the-dragon scenario. I told him to settle down in those moments. I only made him buckle a seatbelt for the curviest roads or when I could feel the car slide on black ice.

When he found the CDs, I told him to pick out one. I figured he'd pick one based on the design on the front of the CD, or maybe one of those famous, timeless acts like The Beatles or Tina Turner. Or maybe he'd recognize the name of somebody a more current musician had collaborated with for a single track.

But he picked out *Green* by REM and asked me to put on a ballad called "You Are The Everything." I knew the song Turd was talking about. I hadn't thought of it—let alone listened to it—in his lifetime, though.

I skipped through tracks until we got to it, and though I felt uncertain about talking over a song he'd selected with such conviction, my curiosity could only hold for so long. "How do you know this one?"

He told me about Cleopatra. She'd wrestled on the CCCC. Word was that Cleopatras was legitimately of Egyptian descent. "She was the most beautiful woman I've ever seen." Turd had a certain tone he took on sometimes. Maybe he was parroting his father or grandfather. Regardless, he sounded old and wise and wistful when he told me, "She's the one who got away."

Cleopatra had been in a relationship with Turd's uncle Padric during an era when Turd was under his care and rode with him from town to town. Padric seeing Cleopatra—Cleo, she insisted the two of them, but not the entire locker room, call her—came with such synchronicity to Turd riding with his uncle that, in retrospect, Turd felt certain it wasn't coincidental. Padric has never taken much interest in Turd, before or since, but Cleo liked kids, and so Turd was a tool to shore up that she'd want to spend time with his uncle.

And Turd didn't mind being used. Even at the time, he wasn't so naive to think that this woman, fifteen or so years his senior would have a romantic interest in him. Still, Turd got to watch her sleep and touch her hair on overnight drives when she reclined her seat and when Padric was too focused on the road to notice. What was the harm in touching her then? What was the harm in everybody being happy?

Of course, Turd wasn't always happy. Padric would send him out to pick him up a soda or a sandwich or to go for a walk, no matter the hour, no matter how cold it was when they got to her hotel, so he and Cleo could get a half hour alone. When Turd came back, the two of them would look like they did after they'd wrestled, a little flushed, a little sweaty, and before he understood the mechanics of what they'd been doing, he gathered the gist of what the rumpled bedspread meant.

And then there was "You Are The Everything." Turd remembered the song playing on Cleo's last ride with them. The lyrics *and you're drifting off to sleep with your teeth in your mouth* carried a sense of finality, a gravitas. Word was Cleo heading to the States for a big money offer, and though she'd half-heartedly suggested Padric could come with her, they both knew he'd never leave his father's territory. The song was broadcasted into the car from a college radio station, on which the DJs touted that they were playing all deep cuts from late 1980s albums. When "You Are The Everything" came on, Cleo said, "Oh my God, this was my favorite song," and turned up the volume loud. Turd was entranced with the melody, with the melancholy that dropped from singer Michael Stipe's voice. Padric was irritated and said he couldn't hear himself think and turned the volume down to lower than it had started. Cleo didn't say anything. Turd leaned up closer to the front of the car, closer to the speakers to hear, closer to Cleo. Her hair smelled of something like lime, citrusy, sour and sweet. He listened. He memorized every detail he could about the four minutes to follow.

By the time I met him, Turd was twelve. Old enough to have crushes, to flirt, maybe even to date a girl his age for all of the holding hands in the school hallways and sharing sodas and closed-mouth kisses dating at that age entailed. I'd been quick to dismiss him as a child, maybe because everyone else did, for the unspoken premise that I was positioned as his nanny. It hadn't occurred to me the sorrow of a boy without friends his age, or even the chance to try to court a pretty girl.

I told him about "All I Want is You" by U2, that song that played in the background of a romantic scene in a movie I couldn't remember, only that a boy named Dylan and I sat on my childhood home's couch, cuddled close beneath a blanket. My parents had gone to bed, and I thought myself so grown up to be tangled limb on limb with that boy in flickering television light. I told Turd how sweet it was when the boy kissed me, microwave popcorn on his breath, buttery hand against my thigh.

I told Turd all of this while he flipped through the pages of the CD binder methodically, like he couldn't reason the CDs were in alphabetical order, or else didn't know the alphabet well enough to intuit that he should flip to the back.

My favorite part of the song was when the subtle guitar strum gives way to the tidal force of the orchestral swell. I remembered the boyfriend kissing me just as that transition happened, and I'm sure it didn't align so cleanly in real life, but I'd listened to the song and replayed the moment in my mind long after the boy was out of my life, long after I truly pined for that boy or even that moment, until I couldn't help but reinvent how it happened, the romance of it equal parts fact and imagination and richer for the interplay between the two.

After Turd found the CD and handed it over, after I'd successfully navigated a sharp curve in the road, and after I'd ejected the REM CD in favor of *Rattle and Hum*, I skipped ahead to track seventeen and let it play.

It skipped on the opening chords. It skipped worse on Bono's vocal and worse by the time the first chorus hit until it was impossible to make out the melody from the noise and errant repetition. I gave up.

We rode on in quiet.

Turd said he was sure it was a good song. He said he was sorry he couldn't hear it.

\#

Turd slept. For all his energy, he was still a child, too, and particularly for those drives that stretched late into the night, three hundred miles on the same empty stretch of road, he'd nod off in the back. And I'd call my father.

I learned not to worry about what time of night it was, struggling to keep track of time zones and differences. Dad always answered regardless, always the TV on in the background, often as not sipping on something as we spoke. I wouldn't necessarily have characterized him as an insomniac, but in Mom's absence, I could only assume he slept most nights in his recliner, maybe stayed straight through the days, only getting up long enough to use the bathroom or get his next food or drink, maybe brush his teeth or shower a couple times a week. Wasn't there something to envy in that? Society would condition people not to aspire to sedentary lives, but what more relaxed easier life could there be than live in the glow of the television? Was my life so different—most of it behind the wheel of a car, squinting to see road signs when they came, sometimes after a matter of hours and through snow squalls? Did the fact that my life might be at risk if I fell asleep in my seat make that life more worth living?

I drove, one hand on the wheel, one pressing my phone to my ear. That was against the law in most states in the US, but I didn't know what the laws were in Canada. For those hundreds of miles without a police car in sight, did laws exist?

Dad wasn't following my career as a wrestler. It was tough to tell the line between apathy and senility when he asked about the Texas heat I'd long left behind or the California waves I scarcely saw at all.

But apathy didn't feel like the right word. Because he may not have cared enough about wrestling to follow where I was, let alone my championships, my storylines— to understand this world of heel turns, double-downs, high spots, and hard-way juice. But he cared about me enough to stay on the line, narrating *Frasier* reruns or movies we'd watched together when I was a kid—*Ghostbusters, Rain Man, Raiders of the Lost Ark*. Who could blame an old man for reliving the glory days of his family—before he lost his daughter to the road, his wife to lymphoma? Such were his attempts to bring me back into his world. And his advice to drive slow and to check my tire pressure against the New England cold may have been misplaced, but no less substantive when the wind shook my car in Canada, driving too fast to be safe, driving as if the next destination were my last.

#

I wrestled Donna Fuse. In real life, she had a PhD in literature, a process that had taken a decade, a process during which her funding had run out and she'd taken on wrestling to support herself, only to find that her job prospects in the ring looked a lot better than her job prospects in academia. A legit six-foot-seven, three-fifty, CCCC sold her as a seven-foot giant, and the absence of any woman on the roster who stood any taller than her chest level, no one questioned the billing.

Donna was smart and sensitive. Sensitive to a fault sometimes, executing a gorilla press slam, then hesitating too long to ask if I were OK.

In any real fight, I wouldn't have stood a chance against an athletic woman close to three times my weight. But in CCCC, where the Franklins had taken a liking to me—no saying whether that had more to do with my successes in the ring or not bitching about being responsible for Turd—I was a budding star. I raked her eyes in old school heel fashion then hit her with a missile dropkick off the top rope to collect the victory.

#

Sometimes on those late-night drives, not only Turd would fall asleep, but Dad would over the phone, too. The first time it happened, I let it go for a while. He was a loud sleeper and it was almost comical to hear him at rest. The next time we talked, three nights later, I teased him about it, but he didn't have any recollection of falling asleep during our call.

It happened more often as time went on. I found a certain reassurance in the sound of him breathing on the phone and Turd's snore, only occasionally audible over the sound of the engine and the car cutting through wind, across pavement. These were the sounds of not being alone.

And though I stayed awake, though I was conscious of defying my own expectations in so rarely nodding off across late-night drives, I could nonetheless imagine myself on a dreamscape. For on these deserted roads, with only the sounds of sleep around me, hadn't I might as well have been sleeping? Might the car take us home without a driver? Was I steering at all?

In these quiet drives, I thought of Ethan and Santa Claus. Maybe they thought of me in those same moments, or that's what I liked to tell myself was possible.

I thought of phantom shooters and stealing shows and the sound of a jackpot hitting in Smoke City. An intimate moment after a show when Machete Betty and I picked shards of glass from one another's skin on a locker room bench.

Think about somebody long enough and you can just about convince yourself you're having a conversation. You can convince yourself you matter as much to them as they do to you, when, in reality, that version of them might not even exist anymore. A new hair color. A new gimmick. A new name. Maybe moved on to another promotion. I recognized in myself a tendency to freeze people I'd once known in time and place, as if they'd be waiting for me, just the way I remembered them, if I ever passed through their territory again.

Breathe in. Breathe out.

#

I could barely breathe in Rottweiler Riggins's cobra clutch. He had a reputation for being stiff and I respected him for not taking it easy on me because I was a woman. Nonetheless, the hold was snug, my neck thinner than he was used to.

CCCC didn't do much by way of intergender wrestling, so there was something particularly nefarious when Riggins attacked me over a perceived slight when my ring entrance started when he was still on his way back to the locker room after his match. It was all a setup, of course, for Padric to save me.

Going from my own wrestler to a damsel in distress felt like a step back, but any storyline with Wooly's boys, and particularly Padric, was as high profile as it would get in Canada. I sold the clutch, not like sleep, but like unconsciousness, face bent under tears of agony, sucking a lick of hair into my mouth to look haphazard, half-dead.

He roused me, just to give me a powerbomb through a table at ringside.

Most tables used for any kind of violence at a wrestling show are gimmicked, partially sawed through to fracture neatly in two with little force, or rigged for the legs to collapse on impact. A table too gimmicked can be a danger all its own, though, for giving way before it's supposed to, when an announcer sets down his coffee mug too emphatically, or when wrestlers stand on top of it setting up for the climactic move. Riggins was sensitive to tables like that. He'd blown his quad going for a piledriver on one years back, when it buckled and gave way unexpectedly. Before the show, he warned crew members, who may or may not have had anything to do with the table we'd use, to make sure we didn't get *one of those sissy tables.*

The powerbomb spot was safe in that regard, though. He'd lift me from the ground and throw my body through the wood, only my weight against the table and only on the impact of the move.

Except, when the moment came, the table didn't give.

There's no factory that makes gimmicked tables for wrestling purposes, no regulation way in which to prepare them. It can be difficult to calibrate for body weight, too, and not many women were going through tables, so the table that might have exploded under a two-hundred-fifty-pounder didn't give beneath my one-thirty-five.

There are a lot of different ways to respond to a blown spot. The conventional logic is to keep going, forget it happened, do what you'd do in a real fight. The answer is murkier when the spot itself is important, though. Driving me through a table was the act of villainy to elevate our story to a new level.

Riggins didn't miss a beat.

I pulled me up by the hair, no whispered instructions, no leading my body, but truly pulling me up by my roots, and positioned me for another powerbomb. You could say I sandbagged him, because I didn't really jump to help him on the lift from between his legs up to his shoulders. But he didn't need any more help lifting me than he did spiking me down.

The table broke on the second iteration. I screamed. My back screamed, gashed—a cut that would require twelve stitches.

The fans weren't watching me in the aftermath, though. The powerbombs themselves—the acts of savagery—were what mattered. The crowd moved on to Wooly Jr. and Walter chasing Riggins with chair strikes.

#

I followed Turd's directions on the road. I no longer felt the need to trail other cars or to double check his work on a road map or think it was a mistake not to have invested in a GPS before moving to another country. Turd had it all down.

And I started talking to him about wrestling. He knew the lineage of championships from well outside CCCC or even WWE, into defunct territories that might as well have done their business on another planet. He surprised me when he namedropped Geri the Giant, whose career wound up peaking in Damphry, after double knee replacement from a top-rope spot gone awry.

It wasn't until later on, well after that conversation, that it had occurred to me he might know to ask about that name, because if he knew that name, he probably knew full well that we'd fought in my last match in Southern Fried Wrestling.

What Turd didn't know were the mechanics of wrestling, because as much as it was a foregone conclusion he'd wind up going into the business, his family had been protective of him too. They let him play at running around the ring and jumping off the ropes, but never with another body to collide with, never off the top rope. Any of the boys who tried to latch onto him with a playful headlock got at least a dirty look from Wooly or his boys. The risk always hung over talent that if the Franklins took something personally, a guy might find himself taking powerbombs through tables on a nightly basis, counting the lights on the ceiling while he waited for a stretcher.

So, while Turd navigated us through city streets back to the major arterials that would take us straight to another province, I told him about how a collar and elbow tie up was less a test of strength than a dance, following the leader's footing lest the both of you wind up tripping over each other and looking like damned fools playing grab-ass on the mat. I told him about taking flat back bumps and spreading the impact against as wide a surface area of his body as possible to keep any piece of his body from taking the hit too hard.

We drove over ice.

I was no stranger to icy roads by then, or even driving over a patch of frozen lake, but at Lake Massequepa a sign explicitly warned *NO CARS – ICE THIN*.

"Trust me," Turd said. "We always drive over. It'll take a full day to go around." He sucked on a blow pop that he'd bought himself at the last gas station, I could only assume using change he'd scrounged from my backseat. He added, "You've only gotta worry in August and July—June if you're playing it safe."

I was surprised at how long it took me to remember what month we were in. I was often as not surprised to hear the year, a trick of growing older, a trick of life on the road. It was February, though, about as safely winter as could be. My adult mind told me to drive around, because if I drove fast I could make up time and I had three days anyway to make it to the next town, and it wasn't worth risking my car, let alone our lives.

But I trusted Turd.

I drove out onto the ice.

\#

The calls took on a new purpose.

Dad was seeing someone. Her name was Marjorie and by the time I was aware of her it was because she'd made herself at home enough in Dad's life to feel comfortable answering his phone.

I almost hung up on her first nasally hello, but there were no wrong numbers when all I did was dial my father's contact from my phone. I asked for Dad and she asked who was calling.

"His fucking daughter."

"What a mouth on this one." I was worried she'd hang up on me. But instead, her voice at a remove, receiver muffled into her shoulder, she repeated me that, "Jerry, she says she's you're fucking daughter."

I could hear his grumble, louder, clearer as he took the phone from her.

"Of course it is. Who else would call me this late?"

I asked Dad about Marjorie, and he acted like he had told me about her months before, when he started seeing her, an old high school friend, reunited at an unofficial reunion after a quorum of old timers got on Facebook and found one another. They'd hit it off playing Texas Hold

'Em. "She got me all in. Took my cowboys with a couple of rockets of her own, you believe that? A woman who could do that—I had to get to know her better."

They'd gone out to dinner and drinks and this wasn't her first time by the house late at night. It wasn't the first time she was there while he was on the phone with me. I'd always pictured him alone on his recliner, but maybe he'd been on the sofa with his arm over Marjorie's shoulder. Maybe he'd taken the cordless to bed with them. Maybe, in its lightest moments across the line, the sleeping breath I assumed was my father's was actually hers.

\#

Riggins didn't make any apologies about having hurt me, even when I walked into the next locker room, the next town limping. The most he offered was to say, *fucking tables, right?*

I talked to Wooly about having him clarify some things with Riggins. Like that we weren't supposed to be hurting each other for real, or at least not more than was necessary to get the story across. Wrestlers—professionals—hurt each other just enough to make it look real, to get the audience to suspend their disbelief. It's not like I wanted special treatment. It was common courtesy that you didn't hit somebody half your size as hard as you could.

Wooly told me I'd have to stand up for myself. He said it wouldn't do anybody any good getting him involved.

\#

I got involved with Dad's new relationship with Marjorie, calling not just some nights but most nights, trying him at different hours, not so dissimilar from the way Dad would poke his head into my teenage bedroom when I had a boyfriend over.

The key wasn't to catch someone in the act, or even to stop anything. The key was instilling a memory that there was someone else there. Someone you wouldn't want to have see—or hear—anything inappropriate.

Of course, he had the advantage. As a teenager, I couldn't well lock my door without knowing he'd knock it off its hinges if he had to. From the road, I could call all I wanted. All he'd have to do was not answer.

But when I called, he always answered.

\#

I talked to Riggins before the next time we got physical. I told him that I appreciated the respect he showed for me by not taking it too easy on me, but just the same I'd need him to lighten up some.

He said he understood.

That night, he hit me with a clothesline hard enough to flip me on a vertical axis.

\#

Days passed.

\#

I taught Turd how to get color.

Blood was going out of style in a lot of places, but it was still good for any wrestler to know how to incorporate it into a match for when the time came. "You don't want anyone else cutting you," I told him. "Even if he knows what he's doing, it's a risk. He can't feel what you feel. And if somebody is cutting you, it has to be quick or everyone will see it. The faster everything has to go."

"You go fast, you make mistakes," Turd repeated back to me a pearl of wisdom. I didn't realize I'd said it often enough for him to repeat it like a mantra.

The key was to cut deeper than a scrape, but not to gouge yourself. To cut at your hairline if you didn't want a forehead full of scars. To trust that a trickle would mix with sweat and less was more because a little could turn into a lot faster than anyone meant for it to, and there was no point getting color if you'd have to go home early before you bled out.

#

I wasn't sure if or when Wooly'd stop booking Riggins to beat me up. I thought when he got in the ring with one of the Franklin boys I might move on from playing the victim, but instead I stood in Wooly Jr.'s corner, and after Riggins narrowly defeated him, he turned his sights to me again, this time for a choke slam on the cement floor.

I didn't offer much help on the lift. Riggins didn't need it. He planted me and I got a concussion.

#

One night, Dad had to pee and put Marjorie on the phone. She was chatty. Objectively, she was probably good for my father, to keep his wits about him, to keep him grounded in a world outside the TV screen and his own head.

She asked, "Don't you ever get hurt, wrestling like that?"

I told her it happened all the time.

\#

A wrinkle in my story with Rottweiler Riggins and the Franklin Boys. Riggins got a partner, a new girl from Wisconsin who's play the role of his sister, Poodle.

Poodle dressed nice. She was presented as classier, but with no more scruples than her brother. Still the mean streak. Still the willingness to cheat to win.

Her debut match, she beat Lucy Franklin.

I learned soon after that Lucy was taking time off from the ring, having accumulated enough injuries to justify stepping out for a sequence of surgeries. I'd been positioned with her brothers to serve as her substitute for the intervening months, positioned to endure big beat downs from Rottweiler to set up feuding with Poodle once the new girl arrived.

\#

Weeks passed.

\#

The way Wooly set out the next leg of the story, I'd fight back.

Rottweiler Riggins would come after me during an interview segment at ringside, only I'd be ready with a baseball bat hidden under the ring and tee off on him, a modicum of revenge before Poodle arrived to come to his aid.

Rottweiler shoved me from behind, right on cue, harder than I'd braced myself for. I flew forward into the guard rail, knocking the wind out of me. I was in a fight. I always was with Rottweiler.

I crawled to the ring. He loomed, steps behind. When I grasped the bat, I swung it up, as hard as I could, between his legs. He seized up. I don't know if I'd caught his dick, his balls, the triple play. But he wasn't the best at selling he was hurt. In that moment, I knew I'd gotten him for real.

The art of wrestling is not hurting someone. You make it look like it'll hurt, but you keep everyone safe. Wrestling doesn't function unless everyone can trust everyone else. But there's more than one way to protect yourself. More than one way to stay safe.

The low blow might have been an error—a bat too heavy in my untrained hands. The second blow to his prone form, using gravity to my full advantage, delivering a blow to his mid-section with all I could muster, threatening to crack a rib—that second blow was no accident.

He gasped for air.

This is for choking me out, I screamed in my head so loudly the echo threatened to leak from my nostrils. Maybe it did. Maybe that's what the mucus was, running from my nose, the tears I was suddenly conscious of in my eyes. *This is for breaking my back.*

One more shot to his thigh, because from his fetal position, his thigh was still exposed to me. Because I was unlikely to break anything there, but it would hurt for him to walk the next day.

When Poodle arrived, she hit me with a forearm to the back. A light enough blow that I took a second to register she was there and attacking me. I was meant to fight back against her, too, but I was supposed to be overwhelmed by the surprise and her force. My first hit back, a punch to her cheek, rocked her. She stumbled back dazed, as it occurred to me I'd hit too hard in this fight that had nothing to do with her. I gave her a wide berth, time to get her wits about her before I came running. Time to get her foot up so I could run into it. She hit me harder after that before retrieving the bat, sitting on my stomach and pressing the wood down on my throat. Too soft. I had to pull it down, while acting as though I tried to push it up, kicking my legs wildly like I was fighting for my life while Rottweiler yelled for her to finish me until the Franklin boys came to my rescue.

#

Backstage, Poodle apologized if she hit me too hard, the way women are conditioned to when they've been hit too hard.

Rottweiler said I could take it.

Rottweiler winked at me, ice to his ribs and groin.

"That one's a fighter," he said.

#

I got a hold of Miles one night. I'd all but given up calling him because he was always too busy to talk to me while away hours on the road.

He picked up that night, though. My boy, all grown up and deep-voiced.

"It's good to hear from you, Ma."

My heart melted. I had my share of men in my life. Only Miles could do that.

He told me about work (*it's busy*). He told me about his new apartment (*it's small*). He was sharing with his girlfriend. I hadn't met her. She wanted to be a songwriter. He was going to see her play an open mic that weekend, hoping to get discovered. It all sounded so naïve, but I'd been young once, too, and chased dreams. What was I chasing now—speeding through a kaleidoscope of fat, juicy snowflakes—but the ghosts of those same dreams in the twilight of my career, my life?

We didn't talk about wrestling. Miles never liked wrestling. Never liked hearing about my aches or sprains, much less the new finisher I was working on or my angles.

"It's late, Ma," he said, by way of wrapping up the call, signaling he'd done his duty, spending ten minutes on the phone with his mother.

The windshield wipers squealed against the glass. I could never find the right speed in snow like this. It was always too much or too little, too fast or too slow. Always out of sync and making the worst sounds.

I told Miles I loved him.

\#

They say you can't go home. I understood that by then. The ache to be in not only a place, but a time that could never exist again.

Maybe that's what home was, more than a house or a family. Home was an absence, colder than the Canadian tundra. The knowledge I'd be just as well off driving forever. Driving until I sank beneath the broken surface of a frozen lake. Driving off a cliff. Those moments of driving or sinking, every moment the illusion of getting closer to a destination.

I cried in my car, late at night, another night, Turd asleep and I didn't feel like making calls. I was alone. Would The Taker come to collect me, a child untended? Would the Taker come for Turd if I didn't hear him crying in the backseat?

Turd was growing up in my car. Grown enough to not need as much attention as I'd grown accustomed to giving him. Grown enough for his father and uncles and aunt to start training him in earnest. On a long enough timeline, most every child grows like that, assuming the Taker doesn't get to them first.

I drove because that's what a wrestler's life was, when children grew and people left and places weren't the same as you remembered them. There was always the road.

#

Padric and I faced Rottweiler and Poodle. The mixed tag team match we'd been building to all that time. The payoff. Rottweiler was the men's champion by that point, Poodle the women's champion. Both titles on the line.

Padric and I dove from opposite turnbuckles, delivering twin splashes on the Riggins kin. The referee made a show of slapping both hands to the mat at the same time. Pins perfectly in sync. I hated contrived spots like that. The obvious choreography of it all. Yet I couldn't deny Wooly's wisdom in booking it. The crowd exploded—a big arena, there must have been nearly 10,000 people, not one of them in their seats, everyone up and cheering. I climbed up on Padric's sweat-slick shoulders like we'd rehearsed and raised both title belts overhead. The crowd grew louder.

#

There was a night I listened to my father's sleep-breath. I hurtled through snow squalls until the flakes looked something like stars fallen to earth. Until I could swear the car had taken flight, and I shot through celestial field, not on earth but in space.

Then I couldn't hear my father breathe anymore. I felt the absence of gravity. No stopping. No steering. I felt the absence of oxygen, burning through my rations every time I inhaled.

"Dad?" I said it once, then again louder. Until I was screaming. Until Turd asked what was wrong, because of course he couldn't sleep through the noise.

"Dad!"

A snort from the other end of the line, like one of those especially loud bursts of a snore Dad'd get sometimes. I couldn't help laughing at the sound of that, the sound of his breathing returned, the befuddled "What is it, girl?" from the other end of the line. And he laughed too. I suppose that's what people do, because out of whatever combination of confusion and hysterics, Turd laughed as well, then asked me how fast we were going.

We were driving fast.

"What is it?" Dad asked again, through time and space, from all the way back home. "Can you hear me? Did I lose you?"

I told my father I was doing just fine. He hadn't lost me. I hadn't lost him. In that moment, it felt as though everyone, everything, everyplace I'd ever left behind might be waiting, ready for my return whenever the right combination of stars aligned.

The next sign we passed revealed we were making good time. Forty-five miles from our destination, hours to go before sunrise.

ACKNOWLEDGMENTS

Versions of some stories in this collection were previously published elsewhere as follows: "The Itch" in *The Hunger Journal,* "The Emperor" in *Punk Noir Magazine,* "Shooter" in *Random Sample Review,* "Stolen" in *Defunkt Magazine,* "Smoke City" in *The Broadkill Review,* "When Santa Claus Came To Town" in *Close to the Bone,* and "Wedlock" in *Rock and a Hard Place Magazine.*

Thank you to William K. Lawrence and the team at Serving House Books for believing in this book and giving it a great home.

My gratitude to Adam Van Winkle and Josh Olsen, long-time champions of wrestling-related literature. Without your earlier encouragement, I don't know if I ever would have written this book. Thanks, too, to my fellow writers who are/were wrestling fans who've shared in my idiosyncratic way of looking at the world and offered camaraderie and good reads over the years.

A big thanks to Chris Koslowski, Mike McClelland, Matthew Thomas Meade, and Quinn Carver Johnson for directly supporting this book. I'll always be indebted to Marjorie Sandor, Harvey Grossinger, and Elly Williams for mentoring me into the writing life I now enjoy.

No book will be complete without a word of thanks, too, to Mike Scalise, Mike Peek, and Will Browar better friends than I've ever done anything to deserve.

My gratitude to my colleagues and students from the UNLV Honors College. This is the first book I wrote start-to-finish during my time working with you all, and there's little doubt my time in Vegas had a big impact on this project.

Thank you to my family, near and far, here and gone. Thank you to Heather, for embracing that when you married me, you married my wrestling obsession, too. I love you. Thank you to my father who introduced me to wrestling and my grandfather who introduced wrestling fanhood to the family line.

And finally, to Riley, one of the hardest parts of parenthood has been balancing my writing ambitions with being a good father to you. I haven't always struck the right balance, but I'm always trying. The first seeds for this book came to me one evening, after dinner, when I took you to the playground and wound up chasing you around the steel cage of the tennis court. You're my inspiration. I hope I make you proud.

Other books by Michael Chin:

You Might Forget the Sky Was Ever Blue

Circus Folk

The Long Way Home

My Grandfather's an Immigrant, and So Is Yours

Stories Wrestling Can Tell

This Year's Ghost

ABOUT THE AUTHOR

Michael Chin was born and raised in Utica, New York and currently lives in Las Vegas with his wife and son, where he teaches for the UNLV Honors College. He's the author of seven full-length books, including his novel, *My Grandfather's an Immigrant, and So is Yours* (Cowboy Jamboree Press, 2021) and speculative short story collection, *This Year's Ghost* (JackLeg Press, 2025). Chin won the 2017-2018 Jean Leiby Chapbook Award from *The Florida Review* as well as *Bayou Magazine*'s 2014 James Knudsen Prize for Fiction. Find him online at miketchin.com.